GHOST MINE GOLD

WALKER A. TOMPKINS

THORNDIKE
CHIVERS

This Large Print edition is published by Thorndike Press, Waterville, Maine, USA and by AudioGO Ltd, Bath, England.
Thorndike Press, a part of Gale, Cengage Learning.

The text of this Large Print edition is unabridged.
Other aspects of the book may vary from the original edition.
Set in 16 pt. Plantin.

LIBRARY OF CONGRESS CATALOGING-IN-PUBLICATION DATA

Tompkins, Walker A.
  Ghost mine gold / by Walker A. Tompkins. — Large print ed.
    p. cm. — (Thorndike Press large print western)
  ISBN-13: 978-1-4104-4319-9 (hardcover)
  ISBN-10: 1-4104-4319-1 (hardcover)
  1. Large type books. I. Title.
PS3539.O3897G56 2011
813'.52—dc23   2011033352

BRITISH LIBRARY CATALOGUING-IN-PUBLICATION DATA AVAILABLE

Published in 2011 in the U.S. by arrangement with Golden West Literary Agency.
Published in 2012 in the U.K. by arrangement with Golden West Literary Agency.

U.K. Hardcover: 978 1 445 88134 8 (Chivers Large Print)
U.K. Softcover: 978 1 445 88135 5 (Camden Large Print)

Printed and bound in the United Kingdom by MPG Books Ltd.
1 2 3 4 5 6 7 15 14 13 12 11

GHOST MINE GOLD

GHOST MINE GOLD

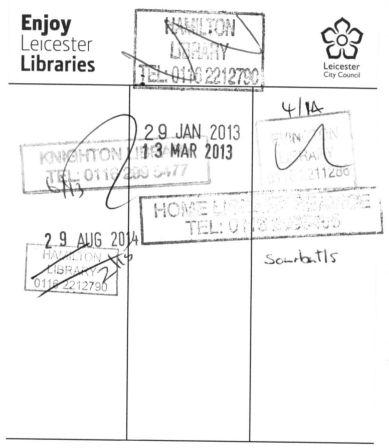
Book due for return by last date shown.
if not reserved by another user it may be renewed.

24/7 - Renewals, Reservations, Catalogue
www.leicester.gov.uk/libraries
Charges may be payable on overdue items

Chapter I
Stagecoach of Doom

Behind the bolted doors and shuttered windows of his assay office, Russ Kern had built the infernal machine with devilish ingenuity. It was a time-bomb whose parts could never be traced to Kern, even if the explosion happened to leave any clues behind for the law of Whiskey Gulch to study.

"It'll work like this, pardner," the gold-camp recorder explained to Shane Pendle, his assistant. The rawboned, sharp-nosed killer rubbed his hands together with satisfaction as he bent over the workbench. "See how I've tied a match onto the key of this here alarm-clock?"

Pendle nodded. "When the alarm goes off," Kern went on, "the windin' key will revolve, turnin' the match with it. This piece of sandpaper I've glued to the side of the box will be in the path of the matchhead, so as to set it afire."

As he spoke, Russ Kern was dipping the end of a dynamite fuse into a bottle of raw grain alcohol to make doubly sure the detonation fuse would light. The fuse was short — gauged to burn in fifteen seconds — and Kern had crimped a percussion cap to the end of the black, wormlike fuse.

The detonation cap was tied inside a bundle of ten sticks of dynamite. The recorder placed the high explosive carefully into the oblong wooden box, where the alarm clock had already been fitted into position with wooden clamps.

Shane Pendle's shoebutton eyes glittered excitedly as he watched Kern twist the alcohol-soaked tip of the fuse into such a position that the match, when touched into flame by the sandpaper strip would touch off the highly inflammable core of the fuse. The box purposely had cracks to admit plenty of air.

"The Ruby Crater ghost mine is as good as ours, pard!" exulted Kern, as he nailed a wooden lid over the infernal machine. "This is set to go off in twenty-two minutes. That'll see the stagecoach well out o' the Gulch."

Kern took a carpenter's blue crayon and labeled the box "CONTENTS — AN-TIQUE CLOCK," addressing it to a jeweler in San Francisco. That would explain the clock-ticks. He put a fictitious return name and address in one corner of the box, even though he doubted if the blast would leave enough of the box intact to serve as a clue.

"Not bad, eh, Shane?" chuckled Kern, surveying his handiwork proudly. "The dynamite, the alarm clock — even the box — were bought out of town. Nobody can possibly trace this to us."

Pendle nodded agreement. They were as safe as a glass of milk in a saloon. There was dynamite enough in the box to blast the Placerville stagecoach to atoms. Hardrock Colter, the grizzled old prospector who had been in Kern's office to file a gold claim the day before, would be aboard the Concord. Kern's bomb was aimed at killing the old miner. It did not bother the recorder's conscience that the stage driver and any other passengers on the ill-fated coach would also be blasted to smithereens.

The pop of a whip and a rattling of wheels on the flinty ruts of the main street outside Kern's shack made the recorder start violently. Hugging the time-bomb against his chest, Kern hurried out of the workroom, crossed his front office and paused while Shane Pendle unbolted the door.

Rushing out under the wooden-awninged

9

porch, Kern was in time to see the red-and-yellow Wells-Fargo stagecoach rattle out of sight around a bend of the mining camp street, leaving a cloud of dust to becloud the shabby false fronts of saloons and mercantile stores hugging the base of the gulch walls.

Panic shot through Kern, as he realized that Grandpa Blake, the stage driver, had left Whiskey Gulch five minutes ahead of schedule this morning. Hardrock Colter would be aboard that Concord, bound for Hornitas to spring the news of his gold strike to his brother there.

"A fortune's gallopin' out of town on Blake's rattler, Shane!" groaned the recorder. "I figgered to hand this box over to Blake just before he pulled out."

Shane Pendle raced down the front steps.

"I'll go saddle a bronc!" he cried. "I can catch up with that stage, with time to spare."

Russ Kern chewed his lower lip with impatience as his assistant bolted down an alley toward their private stable in the rear of the building. The muffled ticking of the alarm clock in the box under his elbow sent goose-flesh rippling down the recorder's spine. His well-laid plans were in danger of blank failure, thanks to the premature departure of the stage this morning.

A clatter of hoofs caused the recorder to jerk his head about, to see a lone rider entering town on a hammerhead roan, from the direction of the looming Sierra Nevadas. The rider looked strangely out of place in Whiskey Gulch, for he wore the steeple-peaked Stetson, hickory workshirt and batwing chaps of a cowboy. The nearest cattle range was in Nevada, and punchers rarely visited this mining camp deep in the Sierra uplands.

An idea took root in Kern's brain as he hurried out on the rutted street, lifting a hand to halt the cowpuncher. He was looking up at a grinning, sun-bronzed face and a pair of keen blue-grey eyes which were slitted inquiringly as the waddy reined up his cowpony.

"I got an express parcel here that's got to reach Sacramento on this mornin's stage, stranger," panted the recorder. "The stage pulled out early, and I missed it. Would it be worth ten bucks to you to catch up with the stage and hand this to the driver for me?"

The cowboy leaned down to take the box from Kern. The recorder stiffened, as he saw the rider lift the container to his ear, having heard the muted ticking of the clock inside.

"It's — it's a valuable antique Swiss clock I'm sendin' to a jewler's for repairin'," explained Kern hurriedly. "Handle it easy, will you?"

Kern was pawing in a pocket of his frock coat for a ten-dollar bill, when he saw the puncher gather up his reins.

"Forget the pay, stranger," said the waddy, hugging the box against his ribs. "I'll be glad to oblige you."

Kern's cheeks ballooned with relief as he saw the puncher spur his roan into a gallop and vanish around the bend of the street in quest of the departed stagecoach.

"This is workin' out even better'n I planned," the recorder chuckled, heading out to inform Shane Pendle of the bomb's shipment out of town. "That buckaroo is a total stranger in town."

Russ Kern would have been startled had he known that the strange cowpuncher was famous throughout the Western frontier. He had come to Whiskey Gulch in the guise of Wayne Morgan, a rambling saddle tramp. But Morgan lived a dual rôle. He was better known from the Bitterroots to the Mexican border as the "Masked Rider," a Robin Hood outlaw whose wits and guns were pledged to the assistance of downtrodden and oppressed peoples.

Wanted in half a dozen states and territories, a sizeable bounty was posted on the Masked Rider's head. Had Russ Kern known the stranger's identity, his avaricious heart would have leaped at the chance of cashing in on the waddy's reward money.

Five minutes later, Wayne Morgan had overhauled the jouncing stagecoach. He saw the whiskery face of a lone passenger inside the Concord, as Grandpa Blake, the driver, brought his six-horse team to a halt, glancing down inquiringly from the boot as the rider handed him a wooden box.

"Feller back in town wanted this to go out on your coach, sure!" Morgan explained, as Blake placed the box on the iron-railed roof of the Concord. "You left early, so he sent me out to overtake you."

The Wells-Fargo coach lumbered on its way, and Wayne Morgan, unaware of the innocent part he had played in an impending outrage, headed back toward Whiskey Gulch to buy supplies for himself and Blue Hawk, the Yaqui Indian who was his partner of the out-trails.

The Placerville stage was dipping down into the long grade of Mariposa Gorge, exactly twelve minutes later, when disaster struck.

A group of red-shirted miners, who had

13

paused in their labors of rocking a gold-cradle on the opposite slope of the canyon, were the only witnesses of the explosion which seemed to rip the sky apart and shake the earth to its very core.

A blinding flash of pink flame erupted from the top of the stagecoach, and when the yellow smoke had cleared, the Wells-Fargo stage was a smoking pile of match-wood, attached to the mangled carcasses of what had been a spanking team of bays.

Marshal Red Royce, summoned from Whiskey Gulch by the shocked placer miners who had witnessed the unaccountable tragedy, poked his way through the wreckage a half hour later. The strapping six-foot lawman shuddered as he lifted a smashed bolster off a bleeding, hash-meat corpse which had been Hardrock Colter, a veteran of the California gold country. Colter had never known what struck him.

A groan from a clump of manzanita brush a dozen feet above the road sent Royce clambering up the canyon slope, accompanied by the swelling crowd of miners who had been drawn to the scene by the ear-shattering blast.

Grandpa Blake, the stage driver, had been hurled up the hill by the concussion of the blast. He was a twisted wreck of a man now,

14

and as Royce sank on one knee beside him, the lawman wondered by what miracle Blake had clung to life.

"What happened, Gramp?" asked Royce, his voice husky with shock and pity. "What blowed up your Concord?"

Crimson bubbles swelled and broke behind Blake's beard as he struggled to speak.

"It was — an infernal machine — Red." Royce had to bend low to catch the dying man's whisper. "A stranger — dressed in cowboy duds an' forkin' a roan cayuse — delivered a box — to me — after I pulled out of the Gulch. I happened — to see smoke wispin' out of the box. It was out o' reach — then it exploded."

Royce's eyes slitted thoughtfully.

"But why? Why should anybody want to dynamite yore stage?"

Death was already glazing Blake's pain-brightened eyes. When his voice came, it was like a fusty exhalation from an opened tomb, but his words were like hammer blows to Red Royce:

"Dunno why. But look — for a cowboy — in Whiskey Gulch."

A paroxysm of coughing wracked the oldster's frame, and when it passed, Red Royce got to his feet, his mouth clamped

15

bitterly as he stared about at the white-faced miners.

"Blake's dead," husked the lawman. "But he's give us a clue to his killer. Cowboys aren't common to these diggin's. I'll catch the killer who put that dynamite on Blake's stage this mornin', if he's anywheres around Whiskey Gulch."

CHAPTER II
ROBIN HOOD OUTLAW

Wayne Morgan tied his roan before "Bonanza" Collins' tar-roofed mercantile store which catered to miners' needs, and trailed his spurs inside the building.

He had already dismissed from his mind the errand which he had performed for the man who had asked him to overtake the outbound stage and deliver a box to the driver. His brain was busier with the job which had brought him to the diggings.

A Nevada sheriff, with a case-hardened posse, had driven the young mystery rider into California, a week before. Morgan knew that lawmen throughout the gold country would be tipped off that the famous Masked Rider and his Yaqui partner were hiding somewhere in the Sierra Nevadas, and a speedy hangrope would be their fate if they were captured.

But sheer necessity had forced Morgan into the open. He and Blue Hawk were out

17

of supplies, and wild game was hard to get here in the gold country, where prospectors and owners of mining claims had depleted the deer and elk which ranged the Sierra Nevada slopes.

Wayne Morgan was strapping his load of provisions aboard his roan's cantle when he witnessed the excitement which spread like wildfire through Whiskey Gulch.

"Blake's stagecoach had been blowed to smithereens!" a turkey-necked miner shouted from a saloon porch. "Killed his passenger an' team. He must have been carryin' a case o' dynamite and the rough road touched it off!"

Morgan's jaw dropped as he realized that violent death had overtaken the very stagecoach which he had seen only a short time before.

For a moment, Morgan considered joining the men who were following the Whiskey Gulch marshal out of town, to visit the wreck of the coach. Then, remembering that Blue Hawk was awaiting his return to their hideout back in the mountains, Wayne Morgan reined about and left the diggings by the route he had come.

An hour later, the cowboy was dismounting inside a brush-choked ravine. As he was untying his provisions, a rustling sounded in the stunted oaks behind him, and a guttural voice greeted him:

"*Hola, Señor!* The food you have brought is in the nick of time, no? I am perishing of hunger."

Wayne Morgan grinned as the brush parted to reveal his faithful companion, Blue Hawk. The Yaqui had a single eagle feather jutting above his raven-black hair, held in place by a scarlet bandeau of Navajo beadwork. He wore a white shirt and drill trousers, and his feet were encased in pliable deerskin moccasins. For a weapon he carried only a bowie knife.

"We've got enough to last us a couple of weeks, Hawk," responded Morgan, dumping the provisions at the Yaqui's feet. "By that time we should be over in Utah, where the hunt won't be quite so hot."

The Yaqui smiled, shouldering the load and disappearing into the brush. A short distance away they had spread their bedrolls in a secluded spot sheltered from the elements, and their horses would be there — the pinto and *grulla* which served as Blue Hawk's saddler and pack animal, and Midnight, the coal-black mustang which Morgan rode when he wore the black Stetson, domino mask and sable-hued cloak of the Masked Rider.

Blue Hawk enjoyed the benefits of a fair-ish education, picked up at mission schools in the past. He was the only man living who knew that the Masked Rider was Wayne Morgan; but beyond that, and the deadly adventures they had shared through the years, Morgan's past was a closed book even to his trusty Yaqui friend.

Despite the fact that every sheriff, United States marshal and cowtown lawman west of the Pecos would pawn their souls to notch a gunsight on either of the mystery riders, there were men in widely scattered portions of the West who knew that the Masked Rider and his Yaqui comrade were not the black-hearted killers the law believed them to be.

Their guns had always been at the command of suffering humanity, a fact which had earned Wayne Morgan the nickname of a Robin Hood outlaw. There was no basis in fact for the many outrages and murders which had been placed on the Masked Rider's checkered record.

Morgan had stripped off the roan's saddle and was busy rubbing down the horse when a drumming of many hoofs startled the mystery rider. He straightened, jaw hardening as his lean, rope-calloused hands dropped to the butts of the twin Colt. 45s which hung in well-oiled holsters at either hip.

Riders were plunging down into their hideout ravine, and were so desperately close at hand that Morgan knew he could not saddle up and reach the camp where Blue Hawk was even now engaged in rustling up a meal from the supplies which the cowboy had brought in from Whiskey Gulch.

Cupping hands to mouth, Morgan gave the penetrating cry of a mountain lion, to warn Blue Hawk to remain in hiding. A moment later, a dozen heavily-armed horsemen galloped into the little clearing.

Harsh yells ripped out as the riders circled Wayne Morgan, covering him with a menacing ring of guns. Their leader, a barrel-chested hombre in a flat-crowned California range hat and wearing a miner's red shirt and high laced boots, swung out of the saddle and approached the cowboy. A long-barreled Colt jutted from the man's fist.

"Howdy, gents!" greeted Morgan, thoughts roiling through his brain.

It seemed impossible that the law could have traced him here. Certainly this was not the Nevada posse which they had outwitted, five days before, in the burning wastes east of Death Valley. But there was a marshal's badge on the band of the gunman's Stetson who now halted alongside the roan, his Colt aimed at Morgan's chest.

The lawman glanced around the ravine, satisfying himself that the cowboy was alone. Sunlight glinted on rifle barrels, as the marshal's riders closed in to completely surround Morgan.

"I'm Red Royce, marshal o' Whiskey Gulch," said the lawman, as Morgan raised his arms slowly before the threat of cocked guns. "I'm lookin' for an hombre dressed in cowboy's duds. You seem to fit that description."

Morgan scowled puzzledly, as he saw the redheaded marshal eyeing him appraisingly, from his spurred Coffeyville cowboots to the tip of his gray John B.

"What am I wanted for, Royce?" asked Morgan coolly. His voice gave no hint of his inner tenseness. If Red Royce said anything about the Masked Rider, Morgan knew that doom had overtaken him at last. He would be riddled with slugs before he could get a Colt out of leather.

"Did you visit the gold camp this mornin', stranger?" Royce's question cut like a bowie blade, into the hushed stillness.

"Reckon I did. Any crime in that?"

Triumphant lights kindled in the marshal's eyes.

"Did you happen to know," continued Royce, "that the Placerville stagecoach was blown sky-high down in Mariposa Canyon this mornin'?"

Morgan's veins jelled, as he tried to fathom what Royce was getting at.

"I came out of the Bonanza Mercantile store this mornin'," Morgan confessed, "and I heard folks on the street talkin' about the blast. What's that got to do with me?"

A high-pitched oath came from one of Royce's men, in that moment. Looking up, Wayne Morgan recognized Bonanza Collins, the rawboned old trader who had sold him his supplies that morning.

"That's the man, Red!" cried the storekeeper. "Remember his face and the hang of his smokepoles. This is the buckaroo who bought grub and ammunition in the Bonanza. I'll take oath on that!"

Morgan sensed the rising hostility of the men facing him.

"What's this all about?" he demanded, making no move to resist as Royce reached out to empty Morgan's holsters of their .45s. "Is it a crime to trade with Collins?"

"Just this, bucko!" snarled Royce. "An infernal machine blowed up that stage this mornin'. The driver lived long enough to tell me that a cowpuncher overtook his stage and handed him a box which later exploded. I'm puttin' you under arrest for the murder of Grandpa Blake and his passenger, Hardrock Colter."

Morgan groaned as the marshal whipped out a pair of manacles and then snapped the handcuffs over his wrists.

"Wait a minute!" gasped the cowboy. "I admit I handed a box to that stage driver. But an hombre in Whiskey Gulch gave it to me, askin' me to catch up with the Wells-Fargo driver."

Royce paused. There was a ring of truth in the cowboy's words, which did not escape the lawman's shrewd ear. Trained to judge character, Red Royce had to admit to himself that this clean-cut young hombre did not appear to be capable of such a diabolical outrage. Had he been an innocent dupe in this calamity?

"Who gave you that box?" asked Royce. "If you can talk your way out of stretchin' hemp, son, I'll be the first to congratulate you. Can you describe the hombre you mention?"

"I'd know the jasper if I saw him again," Morgan said desperately. "I didn't get a good look at him, but he was about your build, wore a gambler's broadcloth coat —"

Royce motioned with a gun barrel at Morgan's saddle.

"Rig your bronc," he ordered the handcuffed prisoner. "We're slopin' back to camp, and a kangaroo court can hear your story. By the way, what's your name, and what is a cowpuncher doin' in a hideout like this, in the Sierra Nevadas?"

Busy cinching the stock saddle aboard his roan, Morgan gulped hard. He had no fear of divulging his name, but his presence in such a suspicious spot would be hard to explain away.

"My monicker is Morgan — Wayne Morgan," he said. "I — I was headin' for the San Joaquin, hopin' I could rent my lass'-rope to some big cattle syndicate."

A few moments later, completely surrounded by hostile-faced men, Wayne Morgan headed toward Whiskey Gulch, with Red Royce leading the cavalcade.

Safe in the screening brush, Blue Hawk had been an interested listener to the proceedings. The Indian had prudently kept out of sight, realizing that the odds were too heavy for any attempt to rescue his partner.

Giving the mining camp posse a safe head start, Blue Hawk hurried back to where the horses were grazing. He flung a saddle aboard Midnight, the black stallion, and made sure that the saddle bags contained the Masked Rider's costume. Whether Wayne Morgan would ever don his black raiment again, Blue Hawk had cause to doubt, even though he knew that his partner was an expert at getting out of trouble.

Then mounting his leggy *grulla*, Blue Hawk headed out of the secluded ravine, his coppery face grave.

CHAPTER III
LYNCH TALK

Night had settled over the Sierra Nevada range by the time Blue Hawk halted the two horses on the rimrock overlooking the twinkling lights which marked Whiskey Gulch, sprawled for a half mile along the pit of the canyon.

Descending toward the town by a trail which led down a side draw, the Yaqui picketed the horses in a clump of liveoaks. Then he headed on foot down a side street flanked by canvas-topped rooming houses and miners' shacks.

Indians were not uncommon in the El Dorado country, and Blue Hawk attracted no attention as he moved among the bearded and gun-hung miners who crowded the plank sidewalks of the town. An air of tension overhung Whiskey Gulch, and Blue Hawk had no doubt but that Wayne Morgan's fate was the cause of that tension.

He soon located the jail, a sturdy, rock-walled building perched on the south slope of Whiskey Gulch. A small crowd of miners had gathered in front of it, and Blue Hawk shuddered as he heard them discussing the explosion which had killed Grandpa Blake and his passenger earlier that day.

"Señor is inside," the Yaqui deduced. "He is still alive."

Blue Hawk returned to the main street. His cameralike memory enabled him to pick out several members of Marshal Royce's posse, mingling with the street throngs. He followed one of them — the grizzled oldster who had identified Morgan as the cowboy who had traded at the Bonanza Mercantile store — into the barroom of the Stampede Saloon, the diggings' largest drinking establishment.

Indians were usually barred from saloons, and Blue Hawk was not surprised when a burly saloon bouncer met him just inside the batwing doors and ordered him to leave.

"Redskins ain't allowed likker in this town. On your way!"

Padding noiselessly along the saloon porch, Blue Hawk was in the act of heading on down the street when he heard a raucous voice addressing the barroom mob inside:

"That Morgan jasper's guilty, men. Why

wait for a kangaroo court to give him a trial tomorrow? Will that bring Gramp or the old prospector back to life?"

A harsh rumble of voices greeted the speaker's suggestion:

"Lynch him!"

"Hangrope's too good for a dirty skunk like Morgan! Tie a stick o' dynamite with a short fuse to him and give him a dose o' the medicine he give Blake an' Colter!"

The Indian drew aside the fluttering saloon curtains and peered into the barroom. A cadaverous hombre clad in a black coat was standing on the bar, waving a whiskey bottle as he peered down at the sombreroed heads below him.

"Royce won't leave much of a guard at that jail tonight," the spokesman went on, his voice thick with liquor. "Only Crowfoot Hawkley, the jailer, most likely. Royce thinks his jail is lynch-proof. We'll show him!"

The man's voice was drowned in a chorus of yells. The saloon mob doubtlessly contained many friends of the murdered men, and whiskey had inflamed them to murderous heat.

"We'll have a hangin' bee before sun-up, Kern!" bawled Collins, owner of the Bonanza store. "Morgan'll be toastin' his heels in Hades for that dynamite job he pulled!"

Desperation shot through Blue Hawk, as he hurried off the porch. The lynchers would probably not strike until the town had settled down for the night, but there were precious few hours left to save Wayne Morgan. A lone Indian against a lynch-inflamed gold camp made the odds look impossibly hard, but the resourceful Yaqui already had a scheme running through his head.

From a livery stable hostler, the Yaqui inquired the way to Marshal Red Royce's home, and obtained instructions when he explained that he had a claim-jumping complaint to lodge with the lawman.

Hurrying toward Nugget Avenue, the side street on which the marshal lived, Blue Hawk skidded to a halt in the dusty street as he caught sight of a sign hanging from a small shack at the intersection:

WHISKEY GULCH
RECORDER'S OFFICE
MINERALS ASSAYED INSIDE
RUSSELL KERN, RECORDER
REGISTER YOUR GOLD CLAIMS
HERE!

"Kern!" whispered Blue Hawk, hurrying on through the night. "The name of the hombre who wants to see Wayne Morgan hung."

Ten minutes later, the Yaqui was hidden in a rose bush in the front yard of a small, weather-beaten frame shack which the stable tender had said was Royce's home. The house was dark, and a couple of circuits around it convinced Blue Hawk that the marshal was absent.

Sweat oozed from Blue Hawk's pores as he squatted down to wait. He debated whether to tip off Royce concerning the potential hanging-bee which an hombre named Kern was stirring up among the lawless element down at the Stampede bar. But the Yaqui doubted whether the marshal, alone, could stem the tide of hostility which was threatening to engulf Wayne Morgan.

Finally, after what seemed an eternity, midnight came, and Blue Hawk saw the towering figure of Red Royce heading up Nugget Avenue. The beefy lawman passed within arm's length of the rosebush where the Indian was ambushed, and Blue Hawk heard keys jingling from a ring as Royce mounted the steps and started to unlock the door.

"Señor Royce!"

The mining camp marshal whirled and stabbed a hand instinctively to gunbutt, as

31

he heard Blue Hawk's soft call. Then he relaxed, as he saw the Indian coming forward out of the murk.

"Yeah?" Royce's voice was knife-edged with fatigue. "What do you want?"

"Claim-jumpers after my gold, Señor," Blue Hawk lied. "You come out to my claim?"

Royce shook his head impatiently.

"Tomorrow, stranger. I'm tuckered out, and I've got a busy day ahead of me. You leave me your name and the location of your diggings, and I'll see about —"

Blue Hawk's fist connected with Royce's jaw like a sledge hitting a steer. The door panels rattled as the lawman's massive bulk collapsed against them. His head lolled on his chest, and his eyes glazed with insensibility.

Rubbing his bruised knuckles against his shirt, Blue Hawk jerked the marshal's keyring from where it dangled under the doorknob. A moment later the Yaqui melted into the night, heading up the hill toward the base of the cliffs.

Moving as stealthily as a ghost, Blue Hawk skulked southeastward along the upper outskirts of the town, until he was above the stone jail. From there he worked his way down through brush and talus, until he had a view of the front of the calaboose.

The men he had seen milling in front of the jail earlier that evening were gone, to seek out the few pleasures which Whiskey Gulch offered. A lone guard was seated at the jail door, the red eye of his cigar ebbing and glowing in the darkness.

With infinite caution, Blue Hawk worked his way along the jail wall, under windows which were heavily barred. His massive fist was closed tight over the ring of keys, to prevent a betraying jangle from tipping off the jailer of his approach.

Reaching the corner of the jail, Blue Hawk stooped and picked up a biscuit-sized rock. Tobacco smoke reached his nostrils as he stepped silently out into the open, arm drawn back.

The rock whistled like a bullet as Blue Hawk hurled it at the unsuspecting guard. There sounded a sodden thump of stone hitting flesh and bone, and the Whiskey Gulch jailer sprawled inertly on the jail step, his chair toppling into the grass.

Blue Hawk glided forward, gambling everything on being able to locate the jail key on Royce's ring. A moment later, straddling the moaning hulk of the knocked-out turnkey, Blue Hawk was testing key after key in the huge lock of the jail door.

His eighth try was rewarded, and the door swung open.

"Señor!"

Out of the gloom of the calaboose there sounded a squeaking of bedsprings and a crackle of a straw-ticked mattress.

"That you, Hawk?" answered Wayne Morgan.

A moment later, the two were shaking hands, through the massive bars of Morgan's cell. The two friends interchanged no words until Blue Hawk, after exhausting his ring of keys, searched the unconscious jailer and found the cell keys dangling from the man's belt. Two minutes later, Wayne Morgan his arms no longer fettered by Royce's wrist-irons, was loping after Blue Hawk into the brush behind the jail.

"You saved my hide tonight, Hawk," whispered Morgan gratefully. "That kangaroo court tomorrow would have put a hangman's noose around my neck, if I wasn't able to produce the hombre who gave me that dynamite bomb."

Morgan listened intently as the Indian described the lynch talk he had heard an hombre named Kern dispensing to the crowd at the Stampede Saloon. Blue Hawk spoke of having seen the name "Russell Kern" on the assay office, and concluded with a brief account of how he had come into possession of Royce's keyring.

"There'll be trouble, once the marshal comes to and finds out about this jail-break," panted Morgan. "But I'd give a lot to take a look at that lyncher who's doing the talking down in that saloon. If this jasper Kern is the man who gave me that dynamite to deliver to the stagecoach this mornin', then we'll have something tangible to report to the marshal."

They worked their way through the darkness to the corner of Nugget Avenue and the main street. There, as Blue Hawk was in the act of leading the way to the Stampede Saloon, the Indian suddenly paused, digging his swarthy fingers into Morgan's wrist.

"There goes Señor Kern now!" whispered the Indian. "Across the street, with the three men trailing at his heels."

Morgan's pulses raced, as he stared hard at the frock-coated hombre who was turning in at the recorder's office and unlocking the door.

"That's the man!" whispered Morgan. "The gent who wanted that stage destroyed. It'll be up to Red Royce to figure out what motive he had for the crime he's trying to pin on me."

A noisy crowd of men left the Stampede Saloon, quieting down as they turned up El Dorado Street toward the jail. Starlight revealed that the burly man in the lead was carrying a rope looped over his arm.

"The lynchin' party!" said Morgan. "They'll stir up the town when they find their quarry has flew the coop."

Waiting until the mob was out of sight, Morgan and his Indian partner hurried across the street toward Russ Kern's establishment. No light glowed behind the shuttered windows of the assay office as they reached the doorstep, and the interior of the shack which they had seen Kern and his three henchmen enter five minutes before was as silent as a grave.

Hoofbeats sounded out of the night, coming from the rear of Kern's place, and Wayne Morgan cursed the fact that his guns were in the marshal's safe up at the jailhouse, as he rushed to the corner of the building to see Russ Kern and his men ride off up the main street, leaving the camp.

Heading back to where Blue Hawk waited at the office door, Morgan saw a cardboard placard stuck into place behind the glass door pane and the drawn blind. It read:

AWAY ON BUSINESS
BACK IN ONE WEEK
RUSS KERN, RECORDER

"Our man has vamoosed for the time bein', Hawk!" groaned Morgan. "I imagine that dynamite job is behind his leaving town. You got our horses stashed somewhere, Hawk?"

The Yaqui grunted affirmatively.

"Then we'll hole up and wait for Kern to come back," Morgan said. "I intend to pin that outrage on Kern if we have to stay in California forever!"

CHAPTER IV
MISSING LEDGER ENTRY

Clad in his coal-black Stetson, domino mask and loose-flowing black cloak, the Masked Rider waited next morning in a talus-littered cliff pocket overlooking Whiskey Gulch.

Blue Hawk had paid a second visit to the mining camp shortly before noon, his white garments disguised by a blanket to make him appear more like the stolid redskins who frequented the camp, begging for trade whiskey and handouts.

With matters as they now stood, the Masked Rider realized that his position in the El Dorado country was doubly hazardous. His description was now common property among the miners who used Whiskey Gulch as a trading center; he would have to keep in hiding at all times, so long as he remained in the vicinity.

Thus, as Wayne Morgan, it would be suicidal for him to appear once more in

Whiskey Gulch, where a shoot-on-sight order had doubtless been issued against him by Marshal Royce. But on the other hand, it was vital that he keep in touch with developments in the mining camp, especially as concerned the return of Russ Kern to the diggings.

Whether the recorder had left town on legitimate business connected with his work, there was no way of knowing; but the Masked Rider believed that Kern had wanted an alibi, in case Royce got wind of his rôle as instigator of the lynching of Wayne Morgan.

The night before, as he and Blue Hawk had ridden away from the town, the still mountain air had carried to their ears the pandemonium which was the outgrowth of the mob's discovering that it had been cheated of its victim. Whiskey Gulch had buzzed like an upset beehive, when the jailbreak had been discovered.

A thousand questions clamored in the Masked Rider's head, but defied answer. He knew that fate had accidentally made him the tool of the dastardly crime which Russ Kern had engineered to snuff out the lives of Gramp Blake and his passenger, a harmless old codger named Hardrock Colter.

But why? What motive lay back of Kern's deed? The Masked Rider instinctively felt that the blast which had destroyed the Placerville stagecoach was only the start of a chain of events which would soon start unfolding.

Accordingly, the Masked Rider had sent his Indian comrade into town on a scouting mission. Of primary importance was the recovery of his roan saddle horse, which Marshal Royce had stabled in the jail barn upon their arrival in Whiskey Gulch, the day before. But the Masked Rider had instructed the Yaqui to take no chances in recovering the horse; undoubtedly the animal would be closely guarded.

Secondarily, the Masked Rider believed that Blue Hawk might be able to dig up some facts concerning the stagecoach explosion, which would shed light on the mystery. Nor was he to be disappointed.

A noon sun was slanting into the Masked Rider's hideout, when Blue Hawk appeared as if by magic around the edge of the granite-ribbed *rincon.* The Masked Rider's eyes lighted with admiration for the Indian's stealth, and he was thankful that the Indian was not a hostile foe.

Clutched in Blue Hawk's fist was a folded copy of the Whiskey Gulch *Weekly Assayer,* the ink still wet on its pages.

"Señor Kern's office is open," Blue Hawk announced, then crushed the Masked Rider's hopes as he went on to explain: "His assistant, Shane Pendle, is running things. He tells the miners that Russ Kern had to go to Sacramento on business. It was well known in Whiskey Gulch that Señor Kern was leaving for Sacramento, long before the stagecoach was blasted, Señor."

The Masked Rider's eyes flashed behind the black mask as he accepted the newspaper which Blue Hawk had purchased in town.

As he expected, the front page was given over to yesterday's sensational destruction of the Wells-Fargo stagecoach, a few miles out of Whiskey Gulch.

"Listen to this, Hawk," mused the Masked Rider. "We ought to get a clue to our riddle in this newspaper story:"

Whiskey Gulch was shocked by the wanton destruction of the Placerville stage yesterday morning. A familiar figure around the diggings, Grandpa Blake, was in the boot when the blast occurred. His passenger, Hardrock Colter, also well known in California mining communities, was killed instantly by

41

the mysterious explosion.

The newspaper account went on to describe events with which Morgan was already familiar, including the jail break. Morgan had escaped jail, "probably being helped by outside agencies," according to the editor. Blue Hawk grinned with relief as he noted that the *Assayer* did not quote Royce as naming an Indian as his assailant.

"Here's something interesting, Hawk," the Masked Rider continued, rustling the paper to get the continued portion of the article on an inside page. "This should shed some light on why Russ Kern pulled that dynamite job:

Mystery surrounds the reason why Morgan, a stranger in Whiskey Gulch, should have destroyed the stagecoach. Robbery of the Wells-Fargo strongbox might have been the motive, but the presence of miners working their claims near the scene of the accident, and their prompt arrival at the wreckage, prevented Morgan from carrying out his nefarious purpose.

Whiskey Gulch's citizenry recall that the dead passenger, Hardrock Colter, had arrived in town day before yesterday.

Imbibing too freely of liquor, Colter told barroom listeners that he had discovered the fabulous Ruby Crater gold mine, one of California's most famous lost diggings.

The Ruby Crater Mine has been lost since the days of the Spanish padres and is generally believed to be non-existent. However, Colter had a map showing the location of the claim, and had come to Whiskey Gulch to record the Ruby Crater discovery. Russ Kern, the recorder, was absent on a business trip to Sacramento this morning, so your reporter could not learn if Colter had filed his claim or not.

Colter boarded the ill-fated Wells-Fargo stage, intending to journey to Hornitas where his brother, Zebediah Colter, is residing with his daughter. Zebediah had grub-staked his brother, and Colter was en-route to tell him of his luck in locating the famous lost ghost mine when he was killed.

According to Marshal Royce, Hardrock Colter's corpse was destroyed beyond recognition, but was identified by clothing.

Funeral services for the two dynamite victims will be held from the undertaking parlors on Goldpan Lane next Sunday.

The Masked Rider laid the paper down and turned to regard Blue Hawk, who was squatting on his heels, black eyes scanning the heat-shimmering roofs of Whiskey Gulch in the canyon below.

"The truth is beginning to dawn, Hawk," said the Masked Rider thoughtfully. "Miners think the lost Ruby Crater Mine is a myth, but Hardrock Colter didn't think so. Maybe Colter was a loco old coot, but at least he brought a location map down to Whiskey Gulch to record."

The Yaqui nodded, his keen brain following the masked outlaw's reasoning.

"Señor Colter filed his claim with Russ Kern," pointed out the Indian. "Perhaps that is why Kern wanted Colter slain. Kern wants the Ruby Crater Mine for himself."

The Masked Rider got to his feet, snapping his fingers excitedly.

"Exactly!" he cried. "By mailing an infernal machine on the stage Colter was riding, Kern saw a way to kill the old miner and not have the murder traced to him. But I'll bet that Kern entered the location of the Ruby Crater in his ledger. I'd like to see that ledger."

The black-clad outlaw fingered his shell-belts abstractly. His holsters were now filled with an extra pair of Peacemaker Colts, taken from Midnight's saddlebags to replace the guns which Red Royce had taken from Wayne Morgan the day before.

"When night comes, we will pay Russ Kern's office a visit, Hawk," decided the mystery rider. "I'm beginning to fear that Whiskey Gulch will never see Kern again."

"*Si,*" agreed the Yaqui. "Kern is even now riding the trail and going to find Colter's ghost mine, perhaps."

With the coming of nightfall, the two outlaws left their hideout and advanced on Whiskey Gulch. Blue Hawk, during his reconnoitering trip to the boom camp that morning, had located the Masked Rider's roan in a corral on the outskirts of town and believed he could recover the horse without danger.

The Masked Rider, invisible as a phantom because of his black costume, left his Indian partner when they reached the town, and headed directly for Kern's office on Nugget Avenue.

Approaching the shack from the rear, the Masked Rider waited to make sure that the recorder's assistant, Shane Pendle, was not there.

Convinced that the office was deserted, he moved furtively up to a back window of the building.

Holding his black cloak against the pane, the Masked Rider drove a balled fist through the glass, the cloak protecting his knuckles and muffling the tinkle of shattered fragments.

Reaching an arm through the jagged hole, the outlaw unfastened the sash lock and raised the window. A moment later, he was astride the sill and inside the laboratory where, only the day before, Russ Kern and Shane Pendle had assembled their grim engine of massacre.

Morgan found the door to the adjoining room unbolted. Entering the recorder's office, the outlaw risked lighting a match, when he saw the window blinds had been drawn.

The tiny flickering glow picked out an ancient roll-top desk which was the office's only furniture. Further search disclosed no sign of a safe.

Using a Colt barrel for a lever, the Masked Rider pried open the desk. A moment's search disclosed the object of his visit — a thick ledger, in which Russ Kern entered the miners' claims and other legal data.

Swiftly, the Masked Rider thumbed over the pages, by the shaft of light from a next-door restaurant which pencilled in through a hole in the window shade. Checking dates, he reached the portion of the ledger which should contain Hardrock Colter's entry of the location of the century-lost Ruby Crater diggings.

An oath of disappointment and rage ground through the Masked Rider's teeth a moment later, as he saw that the last page had been ripped out of the volume. All mining entries for the past fortnight were contained on the missing sheet.

"Russ Kern is takin' no chances of anyone learning the whereabouts of that mine!" whispered the outlaw, turning to leave. "Shane Pendle couldn't double-cross his boss, if he wanted to."

A sense of frustration, of being stuck in a blind alley, bogged down the Masked Rider's spirits as he left the shack, and worked his way back to the hideout where he would meet Blue Hawk.

But the Yaqui had got there ahead of him, and Wayne Morgan's roan horse was waiting there with Midnight. There was no trace of Blue Hawk or his *grulla* mount.

Then the Masked Rider saw a sheet of

paper wedged behind a concha on his saddle. It was a message from Blue Hawk:

Señor — I have gone back to our camp to get my pack horse and our belongings. Will meet you here before dawn.

Hawk.

The Masked Rider grinned, then stiffened as an alarming thought occurred to him. What if Marshal Red Royce, knowing the whereabouts of Wayne Morgan's camp where he had arrested the cowboy the day before, had visited the spot and discovered Blue Hawk's extra pony, their bedrolls and supplies? If so, the Yaqui might stumble into a guard which the marshal would undoubtedly have left to watch the outlaw camp.

CHAPTER V
TREK TO HORNITAS

Lines of worry creased the Masked Rider's face as he saddled Midnight and, leading the roan by a rawhide hackamore, left the cliff pocket which had been his hideout throughout the day.

The sky was overcast, making it difficult to travel through the rugged mountains. Years had elapsed since the Masked Rider had visited California, and he knew he would lose time trailing Blue Hawk, over such unfamiliar country.

He knew, in a general way, the landmarks surrounding their camp. There would be many placer claims where miners would be sleeping, and the Masked Rider knew the danger involved in keeping to well-marked trails.

It was past midnight by the Masked Rider's watch, when there came to his ears the distance-muted sounds of gunshots, rousing echoes from the looming cliffs.

"Sounds like a gun battle, over in the ravine where Blue Hawk and me holed up!" gasped the outlaw, spurring Midnight to a faster gait. "Unless I miss my guess, Hawk's rammed his horns into a trap."

Scudding clouds parted to reveal a lemon-rind of moon, shedding a phantom light over the mountains. Soon Midnight's hoofs were pounding over a well-beaten trail leading from a placer claim to Whiskey Gulch. The Masked Rider recognized it as the route which Red Royce had taken in bringing him back, a handcuffed prisoner, to the Whiskey Gulch jail.

Sporadic gunfire rumbled over the intervening ridges as the Masked Rider spurred Midnight into a gallop, the roan racing behind them. The outlaw tested his six-guns as he rode, getting them ready for a showdown.

Nearing the mouth of the ravine, silence greeted the Masked Rider. Dismounting, he squatted to examine the trail by moonlight. Fresh marks of steel-shod hoofs told him that riders had entered their hideout recently.

Mounting, the Masked Rider spurred off along the south shoulder of the ravine, through belly-deep mustard weed. Crouched low to avoid the whippy foliage of chaparral, the Masked Rider heard a harsh voice lash out through the moonlight:

"I'm sure of it, men. It's the Injun who knocked me out last night and got the jail keys to rescue Morgan."

Ice seemed to slide down the Masked Rider's backbone. The voice had been that of Red Royce.

"He ain't burned a cap in ten minutes, Red!" came an answering voice, down in the ravine. "I move we go into them rocks where the redskin's holed up, and see if we haven't tallied the skunk!"

A moment later, the Masked Rider was reining up on the south rim of the ravine. Spectral moonlight showed him a grim scene below.

Sombreroed miners and residents of Whiskey Gulch were hiding behind rocks and tree trunks, in an arc which blocked the ravine below the spot where Blue Hawk's horse had been tethered, along with their camp equipment.

The weird call of a night-foraging owl came from the Masked Rider's lips. The familiar sound did not attract the attention of the crouching lawmen, but over in a nest of boulders at the base of the north slope, the Masked Rider's cat-keen eyes detected Blue Hawk's eagle feather lifting above a

51

lava rock.

Blue Hawk was alive, then. But undoubtedly, other members of Red Royce's posse were blocking the upper reaches of the ravine. They had probably been lying in wait for Blue Hawk, or Morgan, to return for the horse and supplies.

"You can't tell about Injuns," came Royce's booming voice from a point level with the rimrock where the Masked Rider sat his horse, but on the opposite side of the ravine. "Maybe he's dead. Maybe he's out of ammunition. But it would cost us a man to find out, in case the Injun has a ca'tridge left."

Grunts of assent came from the possemen. One of them yelled back to the marshal:

"We'd best wait until daylight. No use riskin' a man when we got time to burn."

The Masked Rider's lips quirked in a grin as he reined Midnight off into the brush and swung out of the saddle.

Crouched low, knowing that his jet-black costume made him invisible from Red Royce's position, the Masked Rider crept into a nest of rocks overlooking the ravine.

He drew his guns, earing back the hammers as his slitted eyes picked out possemen among the rocks below, several of them scratching matches to light up smokes, in preparation for their long wait until dawn.

Then, without warning, the Masked Rider triggered both Colts simultaneously. Bullets streaked down into the defile, striking rocks a few inches from two of the besieging posse members.

Yells of alarm rippled around the circle of men who had trapped Blue Hawk, as the reverberations of the reports echoed off up the ravine.

"Who done that shootin'?" shouted one of the hombres, who was Russ Kern's assistant assayer, Shane Pendle.

A rustling noise over in the ignota thicket where the mining camp marshal was hidden greeted Pendle's yell.

"It must be Morgan, boys!" warned Royce. "I seen the gun flashes, up on the south rim. None of us are that high up the ridge."

Flame spat from Royce's guns behind screening chaparral, and slugs traced grey smears across the rock behind which the Masked Rider was crouching.

Ducking lower, the Masked Rider called out:

"Surrender, buskies! I can plug every one of you!"

For twenty seconds, a shocked silence

gripped the ravine below. Then Shane Pendle and the other lawman who had so narrowly missed being shot in the back a moment before, leaped into the open, throwing down their guns and raising the arms.

"Hold your places, men!" ordered Red Royce angrily. "That buscadero can't show an eyelash without me pluggin' him. Don't let him buffalo you into lettin' that Injun get away!"

Slithering on his stomach through the rocks, the Masked Rider fired a salvo into the ravine. Despite Royce's orders, the men exposed to the mysterious gunman's fire got to their feet, risking death from the trapped Blue Hawk.

Royce's .30-30 roared again from the north rim, and the Masked Rider had to cringe low as the bullets knocked rock-dust in his face.

But as he lay there, the outlaw saw Blue Hawk leap from hiding and vanish into the brush where the horses were waiting.

A moment later, the Yaqui emerged from the chaparral, mounted on his *grulla* and with the pinto, minus its pack, trailing a short distance behind.

Blue Hawk had less than an even chance of breaking free, but the Indian had wisely chosen not to ride up the ravine, where ambushed possemen would be waiting to gun him down, safe from the Masked Rider's fire.

The Masked Rider's guns went into action, peppering the rocks where Royce was crouched. The rain of lead sent the marshal scrambling for safety, unable to risk opening fire on the escaping Indian.

Straight through the ranks of the posse members on the lower edge of the circle, Blue Hawk sent his grey pony. Men cursed impotently, knowing that the first one of them to retrieve a dropped gun would be cut down by the mysterious gunman on the south rim.

Reloading with desperate haste, the Masked Rider fired a second volley in time to prevent Red Royce from gaining another vantage point from which he could rake the ravine with .30-30 lead.

Steel-shod hoofs drew sparks from the rocky floor of the ravine as Blue Hawk spurred his mount through the group of possemen's horses which had been left further down the trail.

The Masked Rider, his job finished, raced back to Midnight and was in the saddle a moment later. With the roan following him, he skyrocketed along the south shoulder of the ravine, and hit the trail a few seconds before Blue Hawk, bent low over saddlehorn, cometed out of his death-trap.

Stirrup to stirrup, their extra mounts following close behind, the two partners pounded along the mountain grade, the yells of Red Royce's disgruntled posse fading in their ears.

A mile or two beyond, at the fork of the trail which would lead them to Whiskey Gulch, the two fugitives reined up to rest their horses. Blue Hawk had scattered the lawmen's mounts temporarily, but within a few minutes Red Royce would be in hot pursuit, with daylight not far away.

"I was surrounded before I could pack our belongings, Señor," panted Blue Hawk, shaking hands with Morgan.

The Masked Rider nodded. From now on, they would have a dogged posse trailing them, the outlaw knew. Red Royce would hang on their tails even if he had to chase them out of California.

"What do we do now?" inquired the Indian. "Do we head for Nevada, Señor?"

The Masked Rider shook his head and picked up the reins.

"Our work is not finished," he said. "We dare not return to Whiskey Gulch, and my mission to Russ Kern's office was in vain —

the page of the ledger giving the location of the Ruby Crater Mine was missing."

Blue Hawk's shoulders slumped. Their task seemed hopeless, with not a clue to track down. The only certain thing they knew was that Russ Kern would not return to Whiskey Gulch in a week — or ever.

But during the ride out to Blue Hawk's assistance, the Masked Rider's fertile brain had been busy figuring out a new alternative.

"Hardrock Colter was heading for Hornitas, when he was killed," the Masked Rider explained, as they hit a fast canter. "He was bound there, to visit his brother, Zebediah Colter. That's where we'll go, Hawk. Maybe Zebediah can help us out. If he knows approximately where his brother located the lost ghost mine, we may be able to intercept Russ Kern and his men. If not —"

The Masked Rider let his sentence go unfinished, not wanting to admit the possibility of failure. To their ears, down the wind, came the drumming of hoofs behind them. Red Royce and the posse were hot on their trail.

CHAPTER VI
ZEBEDIAH COLTER

It was night in the old town of Hornitas. Gold-mining was no longer a profitable pursuit there and it was content to bask in memories of other days, when the rough miners of the '49 gold rush had made history there.

It was a famous camp, scene of lurid episodes in the bloody career of Joaquin Murietta and other notorious figures.

In a small whitewashed cottage on a timbered knoll overlooking the town, dwelled Zebediah Colter. For half a century, the white-bearded old prospector had roamed the Sierra Nevadas with his twin brother, Hardrock. But Zeb had given up his quest for a lucky strike, fifteen years before, when his wife had died of smallpox. He had settled down in Hornitas, satisfied with a job as hostler in the Wells-Fargo stables. His life was given over to raising his motherless daughter, Arlina.

Tonight the old man was seated before a crackling fireplace, puffing an ancient meerschaum which had been his companion at many a camp along the Mother Lode. In the next room, Arlina, now a pretty girl of twenty, was setting the supper table in anticipation of an honored guest.

"I can't figger it out nohow," complained the old man. "The stage from Whiskey Gulch is twelve hours overdue. It wasn't carryin' bullion, so I'm sure no road agent held it up. And there ain't been any landslides to block the road, that I know of."

From the dining room came Arlina Colter, her shapely figure accentuated by the gingham apron she wore over a simple frock of figured taffeta. At twenty, Arlina was the picture of her dead mother — the same clustering chestnut curls and eyes the shade of a mountain lake, blue and deep and sparkling.

"The stage'll get here, don't you worry about that, Daddy!" chided the girl, walking over to plant a kiss on her father's bald head. "If it broke down, Uncle Hardrock will get here, anyway, even if he has to walk!"

Smoke curled from Zebediah Colter's lips. He had not seen Hardrock for almost five years. His grizzled old twin had never ceased dreaming about locating the legendary Ruby Crater Mine, not since the December morning, seven years before, when he had taken refuge in a cave from a howling Sierra blizzard.

Hardrock Colter had found a human skeleton in that cave — a pile of bones, covered in the mouldy brown hassock of a Franciscan priest. There was a buckskin poke attached to the knotted white rope which belted the skeleton's hassock, and its contents had fired Hardrock's imagination.

The poke had contained an ancient parchment, a letter bearing the date 1770, which identified the priest as one of the Spanish padres who had, under the benevolent direction of Junipero Serra, built the string of Spanish missions from San Diego to Sonoma, lining the California coast like beads on a rosary.

Along with the letter were several lemon-yellow gold nuggets, which Hardrock had brought back to Hornitas to show Zebediah and his niece, Arlina. There were other objects along with the nuggets — rough gems, blood-red in color, crystals which seemed to glow with inner fires.

"Rubies, Zeb!" Hardrock had exclaimed. "Poor quality rubies, o' course, but rubies just the same. My hunch is that this padre

60

was on his way back from the lost Ruby Crater Mine, when he crawled into that cave with a busted laig, and died. There was a crude splint on that skeleton's left shinbone. It had been busted and hadn't begun to knit."

Hardrock Colter had devoted the next seven years of his life to combing the Sierra Nevadas inside a fifty-mile radius of the spot where he had found the skeleton, sure that some day he would find the long-lost Ruby Crater Mine which the Spaniards had worked in the days of the California Dons.

A knock on the cottage door broke into Zebediah's reverie. He bounded to his feet, shouting to Arlina, who was busy in the kitchen:

"That's Hardrock now!" called the old prospector, hobbling on rheumatic limbs toward the door. "Grandpa Blake's stage pulled in, after all."

Zebediah pulled the door wide. Then his eager face fell, as a tall, ruggedly handsome young man in his middle twenties stepped into the room, removing a flat-crowned hat as he did so.

It was Jerry Markham, the young Californian who rode the pony mail between Hornitas and the gold camps up Mount Lassen way. Jerry Markham was engaged to marry

61

Arlina, and he always visited the Colter home when laying over in Hornitas between runs.

Clad in fringed buckskins, the cartridge belt looping his lean waist sagging from the weight of a holstered .44, Jerry Markham was as rugged as a young hickory. But tonight, as he caught sight of his fiancée running in to greet him, the young mail rider's customary grin was missing.

"I — I got bad news, folks," blurted Markham, embracing the girl. "A Chinaman rode in from Whiskey Gulch tonight just as I got in from Hangtown. The Chink says the stagecoach due in from the Gulch was dynamited. Grandpa Blake was drivin', and he was killed. I'm afraid —"

Zebediah Colter's heart turned into a block of ice.

"Go ahead, son," he whispered brokenly. "My brother was ridin' on Blake's stage. We got a letter from Hardrock only Friday, by pony mail. It said he'd be arrivin' this mornin' on the Wells-Fargo —"

Jerry Markham twisted the Stetson in his fingers, avoiding the old man's gaze. Arlina sensed what her fiancé was trying to say, and answered for him:

"Uncle Hardrock was killed, too?"

Markham nodded. "Never knew what

happened. The Chinaman said there wasn't enough left of your uncle to bury."

Zeb Colter swayed, and Jerry Markham leaped forward to assist the old man to his chair. The two had been closer than twins. They had been inseparable partners, up until the death of Arlina's mother at Poker Flats, years ago.

For the second time that night, a knock sounded at the door. The two men whirled, Zebediah looking as if he expected to see his brother's ghost, come to keep his appointment.

Arlina went to the door. She opened it, to admit a tall six-footer, dressed in a coal-black Stetson and a flowing black poncho. The man's face was masked with a black domino, under which his mouth was clamped as grimly as a split in a rock.

Jerry Markham was the first to break the spell which the black-masked hombre's dramatic entrance cast over the room. The mail courier's lean hand shot to his hip, and came up with a cocked .44.

"The Masked Rider!" cried Markham. "There's sheriff's dodgers in every town between here and Mount Lassen, warnin' miners to be on the lookout for this jasper. He's carryin' a four-figger bounty on his scalp."

"Just a minute, please." The Masked Rider stepped forward, removing his Stetson, from which trail-dust fell powdery to the floor. "It is true, I am the Masked Rider. But I bring news of Hardrock Colter. I understand this is his brother's home."

Something in the masked outlaw's respectful attitude, an elusive timbre in his well-modulated voice, caused Jerry Markham to lower his six-gun and thrust it into holster.

"We've already heard about Hardrock gettin' killed in that stagecoach accident," Zeb Colter said. "Did you risk a hang rope to come and tell me that news, Masked Rider?"

Accepting a chair which Arlina brought up, the famous outlaw spoke rapidly and at length, outlining the events which had transpired in Whiskey Gulch.

"Russ Kern is undoubtedly on his way to locate the Ruby Crater Mine," the Masked Rider wound up his narrative. "I thought there was a chance, Mr. Colter, that you might give me some clue as to the approximate location of that ghost mine. If so, perhaps I and my Indian partner can still catch your brother's killer."

Zeb Colter hesitated, his face wrinkled with thought. Then he stepped over to the fireplace and opened a small leather-bound box, from which he took a letter. Arlina and

Jerry Markham were silent, as they saw the old man hand the missive to the Masked Rider.

The outlaw's eyes shuttled behind the slitted mask as he read Hardrock Colter's last letter. It bore the postmark of a remote mining town many miles north of Whiskey Gulch, and was dated ten days previously.

Dear Zeb —

Here's the news you thought you'd never get from me. I've found the lost Ruby Crater Mine of the Spanish padres! I've seen the rubies glittering in the rocks of the crater, and I've seen the yellow stuff lining the old Spanish diggings. I had some dynamite, so I blasted out some ore samples on my own hook. They'll assay high, Zeb!

It was less than a day's walk from the cave where I located that priest's bones. It's the richest strike I'd ever dreamed of finding, and it's ours, Zeb!

Nacheral, I dassn't tell you where it is located, in a letter, not knowing what eyes may see this. But it's near Golden Poppy Canyon, where you and I prospected twenty years back, remember? We were within a stone's throw of the Ruby Crater diggings then, and didn't know it.

I'm on my way to Whiskey Gulch, to record the location of my claim legal and proper. I'm filing it in both our names, Zeb, so's when we're gone, we can will it to Arlina and her husband.

I'll catch Grandpa Blake's stagecoach out of Whiskey Gulch Tuesday morning, and be in Hornitas Wednesday to tell you about it. I thought maybe you'd like to ride over to the mine and see for yourself.

Give my love to Arlina and that young whippersnapper she's lassoed for herself.

Your brother,
HARDROCK

The Masked Rider looked up after he finished reading the letter, disappointment showing in his eyes.

"This doesn't give us much to go on," he said. "But Golden Poppy Canyon is a clue, Mr. Colter. Can you direct me to that canyon?"

Zeb Colter nodded, his stooped back straightening.

"You're durned right I can!" he rasped. "If it gives us a chance of locatin' the skunk who murdered Hardrock, I'd ride plumb to Hades and back with you, Masked Rider!"

CHAPTER VII
GOLDEN POPPY CANYON

Zebediah Colter lumbered away toward a bedroom to get his guns and bedroll, his rheumatism forgotten in the rush of excitement which pumped through his aged veins.

From his place beside Arlina, Jerry Markham spoke up.

"I'm going with you, Masked Rider!" cried the mail courier. "Zeb is old and stove-up. And if this Russ Kern jigger is sided by three gunnies, like you say, you'll need every man you can dig up, if you cross his trail!"

The Masked Rider started to protest — he and Blue Hawk had often handled bigger odds than that — but Arlina Colter was whipping off her apron and running over to a wall where a holstered .32-caliber six-gun was hanging from a peg.

"Where Daddy goes, I go!" announced the girl. "I've got a good pony, and I'm a dead shot. Besides, you men will need somebody to cook for you. It's a four-day ride to Golden Poppy Canyon, I happen to know!"

The Masked Rider waited patiently until Zebediah Colter emerged from his bedroom. The old man had strapped an oak-tanned belt about his scrawny middle, to which were attached a furbished bronze powder-flask and a buckskin pouch. A pair of cedar-stocked Dragoon cap-and-ball pistols were holstered at his thighs. They were relics of the early days when the prospector had arrived in California via the Overland Trail.

"Just a minute, amigos!" laughed the Masked Rider. "It is true, we must start for Golden Poppy Canyon this very night. Russ Kern has probably already arrived at the Ruby Crater Mine. But I prefer to travel alone, with my Indian partner. Too many riders will only slow us up."

Zeb Colter shook his head stubbornly.

"I'm the only man who knows how to find Golden Poppy Canyon, remember!" he retorted triumphantly. "I'm guidin' you there, Masked Rider. I see my daughter and her future husband are honin' to go along. And danged if I don't want them to be there when I notch my gunsights on Hardrock's murderer!"

Argue as he might, the Masked Rider saw

that it was hopeless.

Zebediah Colter was in a position to stand his ground, for he possessed the key knowledge to the location of Golden Poppy Canyon. The Masked Rider saw that the oldster's will was unshakable.

"*Sta bien* — you win!" surrendered the outlaw. "But I don't mind telling you that the Whiskey Gulch marshal and a big posse has trailed me almost to Hornitas. Blue Hawk and I spotted them only this evening, pursuing us like bloodhounds after a polecat."

Colter and his daughter smiled. Jerry Markham spoke up:

"Outlaw or not, Masked Rider, we'll back you to the last ditch. After all, this isn't exactly your affair — even if you are trying to clear your name of Hardrock's murder."

The Masked Rider consented to an hour's delay, while he and Blue Hawk, who had been waiting outside with the horses, shared the bountiful meal which Arlina had cooked in anticipation of Hardrock Colter's arrival.

Jerry Markham loaded a pack horse with provisions, and Arlina Colter presented herself in more suitable clothes for mountain travel — doeskin riding skirt, taffy-brown boots, and a man-style shirt of fawn-colored silk.

A lop-sided moon was wheeling up the California sky, as the five riders left the winking lights of Hornitas behind them. Zebediah Colter, mounted on a leggy gelding, led the way out toward the Sierras, due north. Blue Hawk brought up the rear, his keen black eyes probing the night to pick up a trace of Red Royce and his posse, who must have reached Hornitas in the interim.

All five riders were thoroughly fatigued when sunrise found them deep in the mountains in the headwaters of the Tuolumne River. The Masked Rider noted that Arlina was standing the gruelling pace with the best of her men, her cheeks flushed with the glow of health with which a lifetime in the Mother Lode country had endowed her.

They staked the five saddle horses and the two pack animals out to graze in a secluded meadow lush with bluestem and flowering herbs. The Masked Rider and Blue Hawk spread blankets on a knoll overlooking their camping spot, the travelers having agreed to take a much-needed rest. The outlaw riders did not divulge the fact that they took turns sleeping, so as to maintain a constant vigil against the possibility of being surprised by Red Royce and his men.

The Masked Rider knew only too well that the Whiskey Gulch marshal would not give up the chase, even though a hundred miles now separated them from Royce's camp. Royce was of a dogged breed who would carry on to the bitter end, even if his posse dwindled to the last man.

And despite the fact that he realized Red Royce would shoot him on sight if the opportunity offered, the Masked Rider held no antipathy for the Whiskey Gulch marshal. Royce was doing his duty as an honest peace officer. He honestly believed that the man he knew as Wayne Morgan had been responsible for the dynamiting of the Placerville stage.

Riding alone, the Masked Rider was positive he and Blue Hawk could have left a trail no one, not even an Indian scout, could have followed. But with three other horsemen accompanying them, such a thing was impossible. He could only hope that the Whiskey Gulch lawman had lost the trail back in Hornitas.

The sun was still an hour short of the agreed-on noon departure time when Blue Hawk, on lookout duty, roused his sleeping partner. The Indian's eagle-keen eyes had been watching a smudge of dust on the southeastern skyline, and now his pointing arm revealed to the Masked Rider a tiny row of moving dots, following a rocky ridge

71

miles away.

"Red Royce and his posse," grunted the Masked Rider, hitching his gunharness resolutely. "They're on our trail, Hawk. We'd better hit the grit."

The two Colters and Jerry Markham made no protest as the outlaws roused them from their slumbers. They were in saddle again, pushing on toward Golden Poppy Canyon, with no questions having been asked as to why the Robin Hood outlaw had cut short their rest. As long as they had a comfortable lead ahead of the trailing lawmen, the Masked Rider saw no need to worry their companions.

Dusk found them fording the south fork of the Yuba River, with the country ahead too broken and mountainous to permit night travel. As yet, Zebediah Colter had given no hint as to how much farther they had to go to reach Golden Poppy Canyon, and the Masked Rider did not press their guide for information.

They were in saddle again before sunrise the next day, their stomachs content after a luscious meal which Arlina had prepared for them under the most primitive of conditions. Blue Hawk's *grulla* was laden with a diamond-hitched, tarp-bound pack of foodstuffs supplied by Zebediah Colter, and the

Masked Rider noted it was a week's provender for the five of them.

On and on they pushed, covering fifty miles of rugged terrain interspersed with icy mountain rivers. They avoided mining camps and occasional towns, heading ever closer to the sawtoothed divide, the air growing increasingly colder as they gained altitude.

That night, they were in sight of the great peak of Mount Lassen, far to the north. The only active volcano in the United States was tipped by a thin feather of smoke, and it reminded the riders that Hardrock Colter's ghost mine was probably located in the crater of an extinct volcano.

Then, shortly after sunup on the third day, Zebediah Colter pointed toward the blue-hazed gulf of a mighty canyon which snaked its way toward the crag-lined horizon looming above them, the peaks wigged with glistening snow.

"There's Golden Poppy Canyon, amigos!" announced the prospector. "Remember it like it was yesterday, how me an' Hardrock hunted float ore in that gorge. Made several strikes, too, I rec'lect, but the veins petered out on faults and that was in the days afore hydraulic outfits and stamp-mills. Golden Poppy Canyon was no place for pannin' and sluiceboxes."

The Masked Rider shot a glance at his Indian companion, as they spurred into the lead. Their pulses raced as they headed into the yawning maw of the canyon, its talus-littered floor dotted with the bright yellow blossoms of the California poppy which had given the gorge its name.

A few moments later, Blue Hawk was dismounting beside a pile of ashes which were still warm. The dew-wet grass was trampled by boots and hoofs, and the Indian found a bunch of grass impregnated with bacon grease, where a camper had swabbed out a skillet only recently.

"This could be Russ Kern's camp, amigos," clipped the Masked Rider grimly. "From here on, we travel with our eyes peeled for trouble. Kern didn't dream he'd be followed, so he took his time getting here. But we have no way of knowing how close they might be."

The outlaw waved the others back, as they started to dismount. He and Blue Hawk wanted to study the camp sign, for to their trained eyes, the spoor would tell them a clear story of how many riders had camped here, how old the trail was, and many other salient details.

"We're parting company here, while Hawk

and I ride ahead to do some scouting," the Masked Rider said. "I'm taking command now, and you three will remain here even if I have to leave Blue Hawk on guard with a rifle. Is that clear?"

Zebediah Colter's seamy face mottled with anger, but Jerry Markham knew the reason for the outlaw's insistence that they remain behind.

"The Masked Rider is thinking of Arlina's safety, Dad," spoke up the express messenger. "And he's right. If we all went stampedin' up the canyon, we'd be prime bait for an ambush. We wouldn't want Russ Kern to slip through our fingers, would we?"

Arlina Colter swallowed her pride and backed Jerry's stand.

"We stay here, Dad. This is one case where there isn't safety in numbers. We —"

Crrang! A gunshot blasted the silence of Golden Poppy Canyon, and the girl broke off as a heavy slug hit the smoking campfire ashes inches from her feet and spattered embers over the grass.

"Take to the rocks!" yelled the Masked Rider, yanking his Colts from holsters as he saw a wisp of gunsmoke spiraling from a brush thicket fifty yards up the canyon. "We've run into a trap!"

The black-clad rider riddled the brush

75

with slugs to cover his friends' retreat, as Jerry Markham seized the girl's hand and sprinted for the shelter of some nearby boulders.

Roaring thunder broke out, then, as guns poured lead at the scattering riders from four different angles. Zeb Colter yelped with agony as a slug grazed his shoulder, as he dove into the safety of the rocks on the north side of the canyon.

Leaving their horses in the open, the Masked Rider and Blue Hawk also sprinted for the rocks, bullets whining about their heads as they ran.

Then they were hidden, and the firing ceased momentarily.

From the brush ahead of them came a throaty yell, which the Masked Rider recognized as the voice of Russ Kern.

"Stay where you are, men! They can't move any more'n we kin. As long as their hosses are in the open, they won't get away!"

CHAPTER VIII
KIDNAPERS' THREAT

Moving slowly up the canyon, keeping under cover of the moss-covered boulders, the Masked Rider approached the spot from which he had heard Kern shout.

A few yards behind him, Blue Hawk was fitting a steel-tipped Yaqui arrow to a chokeberry hunting bow which he had managed to jerk off his saddle before taking flight. The Indian was an expert rifleman, but there were times when a silent bow and arrow were preferable.

Keeping close to the cliff, his eyes fixed on the brush behind which he knew Russ Kern to be hiding, the Masked Rider did not see the stocky figure which suddenly appeared on a ledge ten feet overhead.

This ambusher held a Winchester and was drawing a bead on the Masked Rider's back. But a split instant before he could fire, Blue Hawk's bowstring twanged and the outlaw jerked back, his body pierced by a hard-driven arrow.

Blood spattered down over the rocks where the Masked Rider was crawling, and the ambusher's .30-30 clattered down a moment later. Wayne Morgan peered up at the head and shoulders and dangling arms of the drygulcher whom his Indian comrade had shot down.

"*Gracias,* Hawk!" whispered the Masked Rider, twisting his head to peer back at the Yaqui who was nocking another arrow to his hunting bow. "Now we only got three buskies to fight."

Meanwhile, on the opposite side of the canyon and several yards nearer the mouth, Arlina Colter was crouching beside Jerry Markham, her face knitted with worry.

"Dad was hit, Jerry!" whispered the girl. "He's over in those rocks. I want to go to him."

Markham shook his head grimly.

"Nothing doin', honey. Your dad's all right — he was just grazed by a slug. You wait here, 'Lina, while I duck over to the south side and help the Masked Rider sneak up on those gulchers."

Before the girl could cry out, Jerry Markham had left his shelter and was bolting past the horses to gain the side of the canyon where Blue Hawk and the Masked Rider

78

had vanished, a few moments before. A thunderous salvo of shots rang out, as Markham zigzagged his way to the shelter of the boulder pile. The mail courier grinned, as he scuttled through the rocks. Gunsmoke would now reveal the positions of Russ Kern and his henchmen.

Arlina Colter, left alone, decided to act contrary to Jerry's wishes and seek out the spot where her father had hidden himself. She could not be sure that Zebediah Colter was not grievously wounded, for she had heard no shot or sound from the old prospector since he'd dived to shelter.

Hugging the base of the cliff, the girl slithered deeper into the canyon, intending to approach her father's hideout from above. She clutched a pearl-handled .32 Colt, and her blue eyes probed the brush ahead.

A rattling pebble behind her caused Arlina to stiffen and start to whirl. An instant later, a heavy hand clapped over her mouth from behind, and she found her arms pinned to her sides in an embrace that squeezed the breath from her lungs.

Struggling, the girl saw a rat-faced outlaw, holding the blade of a bowie knife against her side. It was Russ Kern.

"Don't make a sound," whispered the

Whiskey Gulch killer. "Me and my men are outnumbered now, and the Masked Rider is a tough man to buck. We're takin' you along with us, for protection!"

Arlina Colter felt the point of the knife prick through her fawn-colored blouse and send a rivulet of blood coursing down her skin. She sank her teeth into the palm of Kern's hand, in a frantic effort to break free from the killer's gagging fingers so that she could scream an alarm.

Mouthing a vile oath, Russ Kern jerked his knife from the girl's ribs, reversed it in his hand, and brought the brass-and-leather hilt of the bowie down hard against the side of Arlina's head. With a muffled groan, the girl slumped in Kern's grasp.

Sheathing the knife, Kern threw the girl over his shoulder and burrowed into the brush. A few moments later he was well past the spot where Zebediah Colter had holed up, and was scrambling down into a small clearing where he and his outlaws had left their horses.

They had broken camp hurriedly, a half hour before, when they had caught sight of the Masked Rider's party approaching. It seemed impossible that the riders could be tracing them, but from the shelter of the chaparral they had seen the black-clad outlaw heading into Golden Poppy Canyon.

Working swiftly, Russ Kern lifted the unconscious girl across the saddle of his strawberry roan. Then he swung up behind the cantle and spurred up the canyon.

"Come on, amigos!" yelled the outlaw boss. "I got the girl with me, and if those skunks trail us, she'll be the first to die!"

Tex Rayborne and Bonanza Collins, two of the men whom Kern had let into his plan to locate and develop the Ruby Crater Mine, came scrambling out of ambush in response to their chief's order. But the fourth member of their party, Blacky Mc-Caw, did not show up. As the outlaw trio galloped up the canyon, they spotted Mc-Caw's corpse lodged on a brushy ledge, his neck pierced by an Indian arrow.

A moment later, the Masked Rider broke through the screening brush, his face going grim as he caught a glimpse of the three outlaws galloping out of sight around a bend of Golden Poppy Gorge. He swore silently as he saw the body of Arlina Colter swaying in Kern's saddle.

"Kern's kidnaped Arlina!" yelled the Masked Rider, turning back and racing to their horses. "They aim to use her as a shield."

Zeb Colter, a crude bandage wrapped

81

around his bullet-nicked shoulder, raced out into the open as the Masked Rider and Blue Hawk leaped into their saddles. Jerry Markham, his face ashen-color with the shock of the news of his fiancée's capture, scrambled out to join Colter.

"I should never 'a' left her alone!" groaned Markham, as the four slammed through the brush in pursuit of the fleeing kidnapers. "If they harm a hair o' 'Lina's head I'll —"

Crouched low over saddle-horns, guns ready in case they overtook the outlaws who had sped up the canyon ahead of them, the four man-hunters pounded along the cliff-bound corridor for more than a mile, without seeing any trace of Kern and his men except the trail-dust which clung to the air.

Then, rounding a bend in the gorge, the Masked Rider threw up an arm and skidded Midnight to a halt. The others reined up, to see the Masked Rider pointing to a flat slab of quartz which jutted up from the trailside like a tombstone.

Words had been scribbled on the snow-white rock with the leaden tip of a bullet:

WE WON'T KILL THE GIRL IF YOU HOMBRES GIVE UP THE CHASE. RIDE OUT OF THE CAN-YON AND CLIMB EL DIABLO

PEAK ON THE OTHER SIDE OF THE VALLEY. WE CAN SEE YOU ON THE PEAK WITH OUR GLASSES AND KNOW YOU'RE TOO FAR OFF TO BE DANGEROUS TO US. WHEN YOU DO THAT, WE RELEASE THE GIRL UNHARMED TO RETURN TO YOU. DEFY US AND THE GIRL DIES.

The Masked Rider pursed his lip grimly, his brain busy.

"This is a trick, amigos!" he rasped, picking up his reins and staring up the canyon. "Russ Kern wrote this to buffalo us into giving up. We've got to catch 'em, if we're to save Arlina's life."

The Masked Rider hipped about in saddle to discover that Jerry Markham, his eyes ablaze and his face muscles working, had whipped out his Colt .44 and leveled it at the black-clad outlaw.

"Nothin' doin'!" panted Markham. "We're doin' as Kern says. We're ridin' to that peak so Kern'll know we've given up the chase. Arlina's life's at stake, and it's the best we can do — give in to the kidnapers' demands. I'll shoot you dead, Masked Rider, if you buck me. I'm that desperate — believe me."

Blue Hawk's brown hand was inching

83

toward the rifle he carried in a hide scabbard under his right knee, as the Yaqui saw that Markham, out of his head with grief and anxiety, meant exactly what he said.

"Hold it, Hawk!" came Zeb Colter's warning snarl, behind the Indian. "We'll do as Jerry says. It's a mighty slim chance to save my daughter, but it's the best we can do!"

For a moment there was silence, as the two outlaws stood checkmated before the guns of their two companions.

Then the Masked Rider reined about, smiling bleakly.

"All right, pouch your shootin'-irons, boys," he said. "They mean business, Hawk. We'll ride to El Diablo peak — but I got my doubts if Arlina will get out of Kern's hands alive and unhurt, in spite of his promise."

Slumped dejectedly in their saddles, the four riders about-faced and spurred back down Golden Poppy Canyon. Colter and Markham were atremble with suspense, peering back up the canyon whose depths hid the grim fate of Arlina Colter. Russ Kern had played a trump card. Threat of bullets from ambush had not deterred them from invading the upper reaches of the gorge, but the kidnapers' threat had tied their hands.

"Grantin' that Arlina comes back safe," the Masked Rider mused, "this has given Kern time to hole up indefinitely. One man could defend this canyon against an army. I doubt if it's possible to reach the rimrocks."

Fifteen minutes later, they were pushing through the brush to where the two pack-horses waited at the campfire site. The saddle horse of the slain desperado, Mc-Caw, had joined the packhorses. High in the California sky, a buzzard was wheeling lower and lower, having spotted the corpse of the outlaw Blue Hawk had killed.

The shadow of the wheeling buzzard was like a harbinger of doom upon the four riders, as they set off across the flower-dotted mesa toward El Diablo peak, a volcanic cone which reared above the meadow two miles to the west. Twin crags atop the cone resembled a devil's horns, and had given the peak its Spanish name.

Leaving the edge of the grassy plain, the Masked Rider spurred into the lead as they headed through the towering rocks at the base of El Diablo peak. When they had reached the summit, they would be in view of Russ Kern's fieldglasses. But the Masked Rider could not but believe that the killer had no intention of living up to his side of the bargain and releasing Zebediah Colter's daughter.

He doubted if Arlina —

Brrang! An ear-shattering gunshot interrupted the Masked Rider's thoughts. A .30-30 bullet had whizzed inches from his cheek, to strike the rocks behind them.

Simultaneously, the four riders reined up, wondering if Russ Kern, by some miracle, had circled in ahead of them and was gunning at them from ambush.

Then, from high up in the nest of mammoth boulders ahead of them, riders appeared. Gaunt, dust-grimy men, astride lathered horses which were ganted from a long trail.

"Lift 'em, buskies!" came the warning shout of their leader, whose Winchester muzzle was still smoking. "We got you covered!"

Colter and Jerry Markham elevated their arms, dumfounded at the trap into which they had stumbled, ticketing these gunmen for henchmen of Russ Kern's.

But the Masked Rider and Blue Hawk knew the truth. Coming down the slope toward them was Red Royce and his weary posse from Whiskey Gulch.

CHAPTER IX
BLUE HAWK'S ARROW

Red Royce, his face covered with a half-inch stubble of rust-colored beard, halted less than fifty feet away. The gold camp marshal studied his prisoners curiously, his eyes leaving Blue Hawk to regard the black-clad masked man at the Indian's stirrup.

"That's the redskin we had trapped," yelled Shane Pendle, riding behind the marshal. "But I don't see Wayne Morgan."

Marshal Royce shook his head, but he was grinning triumphantly, his rifle barrel resting across his saddle pommel and trained on Blue Hawk.

"We've been follerin' a wrong trail, so far as Morgan is concerned," grunted the lawman, "but our ride ain't been in vain, boys. That masked jasper is wanted from here to the Pecos. He's the Masked Rider, no less. A Nevada sheriff mailed me a dodger describin' him and that black hoss, sayin' that the Masked Rider was headed toward the

Mother Lode country."

Zebediah Colter spurred past the Masked Rider to confront the glowering marshal.

"Hold on, Johnny Law!" protested the old prospector. "The Masked Rider's sidin' the respectable element, this trip. We can explain —"

Red Royce shook his head.

"No explanations necessary, stranger. We been trailin' that Injun yonder, and a cowpuncher named Wayne Morgan. Morgan blew up a stagecoach over in Mariposa Canyon several days ago, and —"

The Masked Rider saw his chance at that moment, and took it. Wheeling Midnight, the black-clad outlaw rolled his spurs and the magnificent black stallion bolted into a cleft between two giant boulders as if flung by a catapult.

Red Royce yelled in dismay and whipped up his rifle, but held his fire when he saw that Zebediah Colter was in line with the bullet. The shift of the rifle gave Blue Hawk his chance, and he again sent his *grulla* rocketing after the Masked Rider, to vanish in the rocks.

It was a mad gamble, but the two outlaws knew that certain death by hanging awaited them if they were arrested and handcuffed.

Gunshots rocked the morning air and bullets slammed and caromed about them, as they sent their ponies hurtling through the heavy rocks.

Red Royce and his men came streaming down the slope of El Diablo peak, guns blazing. But their horses were exhausted from a night of travel, whereas the escaping outlaws had the advantage of being on fresh mounts.

Soon the bullets began to fall short, as the Masked Rider and his Indian partner shot out across the mountain meadow toward the Sierra Nevadas, beyond effective rifle range.

Heading straight east, the two outlaws made for the canyon-gashed slopes of the range, a half mile south of the vast opening of Golden Poppy Canyon from which they had just come.

Glancing behind, the Masked Rider relaxed as he saw Red Royce and his men fanned out across the grassy mesa, spurring their jaded mounts to the chase. The Whiskey Gulch posse had seemingly forgotten the existence of Zebediah Colter and Jerry Markham, for those two had resumed their way up El Diablo peak to carry out Russ Kern's orders.

Once lost in the maze of tangled uplands, the Masked Rider and Blue Hawk reined up to let their horses rest.

"That was a close one," panted the outlaw, removing his mask and black Stetson and swabbing sweat from his face. "Anyway, we're free now to trail Kern and try to help the girl."

They pushed down a canyon which intersected the Golden Poppy, and a half hour later were back to the spot where Kern had left his warning message on the quartz outcrop.

"I'm not worrying about Royce being able to trail us in this wild country, with a thousand canyons to explore," the Masked Rider said, replacing his domino and Stetson. "But his arrival complicates things."

"Meaning what, Señor?" asked the Yaqui, as they headed on up the canyon, following Kern's trail.

"Meaning this — that Kern will see Zebediah and Markham up on El Diablo peak, but not *us!* Kern will guess we're trailing him down this canyon, probably, and do away with the girl. If he hasn't already."

Less than a mile beyond the quartz rock with its grim message, the two riders halted before an oblong of rocks placed near the trailside and surmounted by a flat slab of volcanic lava. Scratched with a knife-tip on the lava were two words:

"A grave!" gasped Blue Hawk. "Señor Kern killed the señorita, and got her name off the brass studs which spelled it on her belt."

The Masked Rider grinned bitterly.

"I don't think so," he said, dismounting to inspect the improvised tombstone. "This is a crude trick to make us think the girl is buried here, Hawk. They haven't had time to dig even a shallow grave. This is a ruse to delay pursuit while we attempt to exhume Arlina's corpse, Hawk. If they'd killed her, Kern would have dumped her body into the brush somewhere."

They pushed on, both hoping against hope that the Masked Rider's deduction was true. Kern had been gambling on the possibility that his warning message would be ignored.

Studying trail sign, the two partners pushed on. Golden Poppy Canyon was gaining altitude at a steep pitch now, and the brush and rocks which lined the pit of the gorge would make an ideal place for Kern's men to hole up and attempt to ambush pursuing riders.

Noon sunlight was shafting into the canyon, when the Masked Rider rounded a sharp bend in the gorge, Blue Hawk at his stirrup.

There, both men halted their mounts, as they stared with dismay at the blank wall of stone which confronted them.

A hundred feet of sheer granite blocked the upper end of Golden Poppy Canyon, the rimrocks curving to join the blind end of the gulch.

Then, lowering their eyes, the outlaws caught sight of three saddle horses and two packmules, stripped of their rigs and picketed in a patch of grama grass, at the base of the cliff.

A glint of sunlight on some polished surface drew the Masked Rider's gaze up the frowning cliff to where the granite rim met the blue sky.

Blue Hawk saw the man who squatted on the cliff-brink at the same instant. The man's steeple-crowned sombrero and head and shoulders were visible above the rimrock, and he had a pair of field glasses to his eyes. It had been sunlight glinting on the polished lenses of the binoculars which had attracted the Masked Rider's attention.

"It's one of Kern's men," he whispered, drawing a .45 from its holster and earing back the hammer. "He's got those glasses focussed on El Diablo Peak to see if we're up there yet. That may mean that Arlina Colter is still alive."

The Masked Rider knew it would be a matter of mere seconds before the man on the cliff rim would lower his gaze and spot them in the canyon below. The Masked Rider's gun was ready to meet the attack of the lookout, when showdown came. He could not risk giving the sentinel a chance to scuttle out of sight behind the skyline.

"Wait, Señor!" whispered Blue Hawk, jerking a steel-tipped arrow from the otter-skin quiver which was strapped to his back. "If you shoot, it will reach the ears of Señor Kern and the others, and they would surely murder the girl. I have a better plan."

The Masked Rider grinned and thrust his gun into leather, as he saw Blue Hawk fitting an arrow to the sturdy bow.

Even as the Yaqui tensed the bowstring, the feathered arrow nestling his coppery cheek, the man on the cliff far above them lowered his glasses and glanced down into the gorge.

They saw the outlaw jerk erect, as he caught sight of them. Leaping to his feet, the killer yanked a six-gun from holster, at the same time opening his mouth to yell an alarm.

Twang! Blue Hawk released his bowstring.

Too fast for the eye to follow, a feathered shaft sped toward the rim.

For an instant, the Masked Rider thought that Blue Hawk's infallible aim had gone awry, due to the sharp upward angle.

Then he saw the six-gun drop from the outlaw's nerveless hand, and he saw Blue Hawk's arrow, imbedded for half its length in the outlaw's chest.

The gunman's knees buckled like rubber hinges. For a moment, he tottered on the granite ledge, and then fell face forward into space.

The dead man struck the floor of the canyon with a sickening crash and bounced three feet before sprawling, a mangled mass of broken flesh and bone, in the grass a few yards from the startled saddle horses.

Dismounting swiftly, the two mystery riders hurried across the clearing and paused, staring down at the crushed human wreckage. The shattered field-glasses still hung by a thong about the dead man's neck.

"This is the storekeeper who run the Bonanza tradin' post in Whiskey Gulch," said the Masked Rider. "Collins, who identified me to Red Royce as the cowboy who visited that gold camp. Apparently he was workin' in cahoots with Kern, and came here to help develop that gold mine of

Hardrock Colter's."

Blue Hawk peered up the sheer, beetling expanse of the cliff above them.

"How did this hombre get up to the rim-rock, Señor?" queried the Yaqui puzzledly. "Nothing but a fly could crawl up this cliff!"

CHAPTER X
DEAD MAN'S SOCKS

How, indeed, had Blue Hawk's victim reached the high rim of the cliff? The Masked Rider saw no answer to the riddle, as he backed off to survey the marble-smooth face of Golden Poppy Canyon's blind end.

"Look, Señor!" exclaimed Blue Hawk "Here are the tracks of Señor Kern and his men. They used no cave to disappear!"

It was true. Even for a tenderfoot, the story told in the boot tracks at the base of the cliff was plain to read. After dismounting and unsaddling their horses, Russ Kern and his henchmen had walked across a patch of smooth sand to the very bottom of the cliff.

And there the trail ended — as surely as if Kern's party had taken wings!

For ten minutes, the two outlaws studied the cliff, walking back to the bend of the canyon to get a clear perspective of the entire scarp.

It was smooth and bare, except for occasional ledges and outjutting brush which were too far above the floor of the canyon to have given the vanished outlaws any means of climbing.

There were no toe-holds chiseled out of the rock; no sign of a dangling rope or a ladder of any sort. The means by which Kern and his men had reached the top of the cliff seemed impossible of explanation. And yet they had the corpse of Blue Hawk's victim to show that men *had* gained the lofty rimrock, a hundred and twenty feet overhead.

"We're getting nowhere closer to a solution, Hawk," the Masked Rider said. "But your sharp-shooting with bow and arrow has given me an idea. I think a dead man's socks will enable us to follow this storekeeper's footsteps. Wait and see."

Frowning curiously, Blue Hawk saw his comrade walk over to the corpse of the Whiskey Gulch trader and jerk off his hobnailed boots. As the Masked Rider had surmised, the dead storekeeper wore thick woolen socks, of a type worn with high mountain boots.

Stripping the socks from the corpse's feet, the Masked Rider walked over to a shady spot and commenced unraveling the tough woolen yarn. Blue Hawk followed suit with the remaining sock, and after a quarter-hour's time the two outlaws had a pile of unraveled yarn strung out on the ground, looped in wide coils to prevent the cord snarling up.

"I do not *sabe*, Señor," protested Blue Hawk. "This yarn is but a spider web. Do you think we can climb this cliff on such flimsy stuff?"

The Masked Rider grinned. He pointed up the cliff to where a sturdy oak sapling had taken root in a ledge.

"Look at the oak scrub, thirty feet above us, Hawk," instructed the Robin Hood outlaw enigmatically. "Do you see anything there, my sharp-eyed amigo?"

Blue Hawk squinted hard at the oak bush, then grinned sheepishly at a detail which had escaped him theretofore.

"A scrap of cloth, caught on the bush," the Indian said.

"Yes — a piece of fawn-colored silk," the Masked Rider replied. "When I spotted that tatter of cloth, I knew it came from Arlina Colter's blouse. It means that she was drawn up this cliff by some means or other — the same way that Russ Kern got out of this blind canyon. If he can go that way, so can we."

As he spoke, the Masked Rider removed a slender arrow from Blue Hawk's quiver. To the shaft, a few inches below the steel point, the outlaw tied one end of the woolen yarn he had unraveled from Bonanza Collins' socks.

"There's plenty of yardage in this yarn to do the trick I have in mind," the Masked Rider said. "See how good your marksmanship is with that huntin' bow, Hawk. I want you to loop this yarn over that oak bush."

The Yaqui's impassive face gave no hint of his inner excitement, as he got wise to the Masked Rider's plan for scaling the cliff.

Fitting the arrow to his bowstring, Blue Hawk took a position below and a few feet to the left of the protruding bush thirty feet overhead, and tensed the bow slightly.

Releasing the bowstring, Blue Hawk saw the arrow hurtle skyward, trailing the sock yarn behind it in a tenuous line. Then, some forty feet overhead, the arrow wavered and came to a stop.

Gravity, aided by the steel tip of the arrow, brought the shaft plummeting groundward, to the right of the protruding oak bush. Yarn paid out swiftly from the pile on the ground, and when the arrow clattered earthward at Blue Hawk's feet, a double line of yarn connected the ground with the oak scrub overhead.

Untying the yarn, Blue Hawk turned to see that the Masked Rider had gone over to Russ Kern's saddle and unbuckled a coiled lariat from the pommel.

Shaking out the coil, the Masked Rider tied the end of the yarn through the brass honda, and their scheme was ready to set in operation.

"This wool is strong," the Masked Rider said, beginning to pull one end of the yarn string. "It should support the weight of this lass' rope."

As the Masked Rider pulled on the yarn, the braided rawhide reata was drawn straight up toward the oak bush.

"Go back to where Midnight is standing, and keep watch, Hawk," ordered the Masked Rider, when the lariat had reached the foliage of the ledge oak. "Russ Kern's somewhere beyond that rimrock, and we can't take any chances of his discovering us down here."

The lariat was of standard thirty-five-foot length, so the Masked Rider knew it would not reach double from the ground to the oak scrub. Accordingly, he obtained another rope from one of the outlaw's saddles and knotted them together.

A few minutes later, while Blue Hawk kept his eyes trained on the rimrock against the possibility of Kern's return to investigate the absence of his sentinel, the Masked Rider was twisting the lariat together to form a thick rope leading up the face of the cliff as far as the oak scrub.

"I'll test this out first, Hawk," the outlaw called softly to his henchman. "I'll bet anything that this plan works slicker'n bear grease."

Gripping the twisted lariat firmly, the Masked Rider drew the rope taut. A moment later he was climbing, his spike-heeled cowboots walking up the vertical cliff, his weight amply borne by the sturdy oak.

Blue Hawk grinned as he saw his master gain the ledge where the oak had taken root. Running forward, Blue Hawk gripped the dangling reata and swarmed hand-over-hand up the cliff with agility.

"So far, so good," panted the Masked Rider, when Blue Hawk joined him on the narrow ledge. "There's a protruding knob of rock twenty feet above us, and a ledge leaning up toward the rim. I reckon we're as good as up."

Once more Blue Hawk got his bow and arrow in operation, this time looping the yarn thread over a jutting chunk of granite which broke the smooth face of the cliff. While the Indian was busy drawing the reata around the knob of rock, the Masked Rider plucked the fragment of Arlina Colter's blouse from the limb of the oak and pocketed it, for luck.

The next leg of their climb was more perilous, for there was always the risk of the rope slipping from its precarious purchase. Within twenty minutes, however, Blue Hawk had gained the perch, going up first because of his lighter weight.

This time, the Indian pulled up the Masked Rider, to save time. His back muscles bulged and rippled like snakes under his tawny brown skin, his moccasins gripping the narrow protrusion of granite like a lizard's feet.

As the Masked Rider had pointed out, a ledge slanted up the cliff, enabling them to crawl within ten feet of the rim.

From there, the Masked Rider was able to lasso a lightning-shattered stump of a pine tree.

Panting like landed fish, the two outlaws climbed the remaining height and scrambled out on the level crest of the cliff.

The Masked Rider clutched a six-gun as he got to his feet, scanning the territory beyond the rimrock in quest of Russ Kern or his remaining partner.

They had a breath-taking view of the Sierra Nevada divide, stretching off and away to meet the craggy skyline to east. Of Kern, Arlina, and the other outlaw they saw no trace.

Then, a few yards away from the cliff edge, the partners saw a pile of what seemed to be stovewood. Boot prints led to the heap, and the Masked Rider scowled curiously as he saw that the ax-hewn sticks of wood were connected at either end with sturdy hemp rope.

"A rope ladder!" exclaimed the Robin Hood outlaw. "See how one end is anchored to those two pine trees yonder? The rungs are made of short chunks of wood. This is how Kern scaled the cliff. After they got the girl up here, they dragged the rope ladder up after them."

Blue Hawk circled the piled-up ladder, examining the knotted ropes curiously.

"This rope is fairly new, but some of the rungs are very old," commented the Indian. "The puzzle still remains — how did Russ Kern anchor this ladder up here in the first place?"

The Masked Rider grinned, hitching his cartridge belts.

"I imagine Hardrock Colter made this

ladder," he explained. "He probably left it dangling over the cliff before he left for Whiskey Gulch to record his claim, knowing that no one was likely to do any prospecting in Golden Poppy Canyon, and find the ladder. I imagine the original ladder left by the Spanish padres was here when Hardrock Colter found it, which accounts for the old wooden rungs you see there. The rungs which were decayed beyond the point of safety, Colter replaced with fresh wood."

Leaving the piled-up rope ladder behind, the two outlaws headed toward a nearby fringe of mountain oak and manzanita. Behind them, they could see the long, crooked gulf of Golden Poppy Canyon snaking down the foothills, with El Diablo peak far in the distance beyond the mesa valley. At this moment, Jerry Markham and Zeb Colter were probably on that peak.

A moment later, breaking cautiously through the rimming brush, the Masked Rider gasped with astonishment at what lay beyond the chaparral.

Almost at their feet was a deep pothole in the Sierra Nevadas, funneling down to lose itself in the haze-filled depths. The circular chasm was at least a mile in extent, surrounded by jagged crags which would be impossible to scale, even by a bighorn goat.

Near at hand, sunlight picked out crimson lights in the rock, like embedded bits of red glass.

"Rubies!" whispered the Masked Rider, gripping Blue Hawk's sinewy arm. "This is Ruby Crater, Hawk — the burned out core of a dead volcano. And somewhere close, we ought to find that lost gold mine of Hardrock Colter's. The Ruby Crater diggings of the Spanish padres!"

The Yaqui nodded grimly.

"We must not forget," he reminded, "that Russ Kern has reached the mine before us. If he sees us first, Señor, our lives are not worth a plugged peseta."

Chapter XI
Captive in Ruby Crater

As Arlina Colter groped her way back to consciousness, she found herself roped to the sturdy back of Russ Kern. Opening her eyes, the girl was puzzled to see that the outlaw was climbing the sheer face of a cliff wall, for far below her she saw the outlaws' horses and Kern's two henchmen, peering up at their climbing leader.

Fighting off dizziness, the girl had little memory of reaching the top, or of seeing Kern's men climb the rope ladder behind them, making two trips to bring up the supplies carried by the packmules. When she revived for a second time, she found herself seated in a crude redwood chair, arms tied behind her back, and ropes binding her knees and ankles to the thick legs of the chair.

A low mutter of men's voices reached the girl's throbbing ears, as she peered about her. She was in a small, one-roomed shack walled with heavy square-hewn logs and chinked with rock moss.

A crude door, on pivots instead of hinges, was partially open, admitting a bar of sunlight. Peering through the door, the girl saw Russ Kern and Tex Rayborne standing outside, consulting a sheet of paper which gleamed blindingly in the sun.

Arlina Colter had no way of knowing that the paper was a sheet torn from the Whiskey Gulch recorder's ledger, and that it bore the mining claim of her murdered uncle, Hardrock Colter. The information Colter had filed with Kern had given the location of the lost Ruby Crater Mine, and had been Kern's guide in reaching this remote spot in the Sierras.

"The mine can't be far off, Tex," Kern was saying, his vulturelike face flushed with greed. "Everything's been like it says here on Colter's minin' claim — the Golden Poppy Canyon and that rope ladder o' hisn danglin' down the cliff, and this here cabin which the Spaniards built. The mine tunnel is down toward the crater wall, a thousand yards from the shack, accordin' to this."

"Let's take a *pasear* down there, then!" exclaimed Rayborne, dry-washing his hands excitedly. "With Bonanza Collins guardin' the canyon, and us havin' drawed up that rope ladder, we're safe enough."

Gathering breath in her lungs, Arlina Colter cried out tremulously:

"What am I doing here? Let me loose."

Russ Kern and Tex Rayborne grinned wolfishly as they heard their prisoner cry out from inside the shack. Striding up to the doorway, they ducked under the time-beaten lintel and stood spread-legged on the threshold, staring at the heavily bound girl. Arlina's chin was thrust out defiantly, and contempt had replaced the fear in her blue eyes.

"You'll stay put for the rest o' the day, at least, my perty young filly!" leered Kern. "You're our bargainin' power, just in case the Masked Rider and his pards get ideas about keepin' us penned up in Ruby Crater."

So saying, Kern wheeled about and headed out of range of the girl's vision, Rayborne following him after a last bold, leering glance in her direction.

For several minutes, Arlina struggled with her bonds, and finally gave up the task as hopeless. The knotted rope was torturing her flesh, cutting the circulation from her limbs.

She glanced about, her pupils widened in the murk so that she could make out the

108

supplies — food, ammunition, and blankets — which the outlaws had brought with them.

Then, twisting her head about to look behind her, Arlina Colter gasped.

A human skeleton was seated in a redwood chair like her own, in front of a crude ax-hewn table immediately behind her.

Sweat streamed from the girl's pores, but she overcame her initial horror at the gruesome sight. The skeleton had sagged forward over the table, head cradled on bony arms. Then the girl made out interesting details about the skeleton. The skull was partially covered by a rusty helmet, its visor lifted. The ribs were visible behind a corslet of tarnished armor, and dangling from the skeleton's waist was a sword of Toledo steel, its tip touching the earthen floor of the cabin.

"A Spanish *conquistador!*" breathed the girl, interest making her forget her own perilous situation. "This man must have been one of the original discoverers of the Ruby Crater Mine."

How the Spaniard had died, Arlina could not guess, but the *conquistador*'s corpse had been toppled over this musty, dust-covered table for two or three centuries, she judged. Her Uncle Hardrock had not bothered to disturb the Spaniard's bones, when he had visited Ruby Crater a few weeks before.

Suddenly an idea soared into the girl's head as her eye was drawn to a glitter of sunlight on the sword dangling from the skeleton's belt.

Throwing her weight forward, Arlina was able to tilt the chair legs off the floor and balance herself on the balls of her feet. Then, inching her bootsoles about, she managed to face the corner of the table where the skeleton was slumped.

Inch by inch, the plucky girl worked her way toward the dangling sword. Finally she had brought the ropes which held her knees to the chair-legs, a half inch from the keen two-edged blade.

As hope of escape shot through the girl, she jiggled the chair forward, pressing the ropes against the edge of the sword. The golden hilt of the weapon, encrusted with jewels pushed against the Spaniard's armor and came to a halt.

The next ten minutes were a dragging eternity to Arlina Colter, as she jerked her body in the chair and, in so doing, rubbed her bonds against the rigid edge of the blade.

Despite the centuries which had elapsed since the Spaniard had died, the Toledo blade still held its keen edge. Infinitesimal strands parted one by one in the rope, with each lunge she made against the blade.

Then, when it seemed that her jaded body did not have the strength to move again, she felt the rope part under the jerky sawing motion.

Circulation warmed the girl's ankles as the tightly-bound ropes slowly unraveled. Soon she was able to kick her booted legs free of the ropes, and felt them unwind to ease the pressure on her arms.

It was agonizingly slow work, pulling her arms loose to the point where she could get a hand busy untying the main knot of her bonds. At any moment Russ Kern and his partner might return from their exploring trip of the crater.

But finally Arlina Colter stood free, spent and gasping with exertion.

"Thanks, Señor!" whispered the girl, stooping over to pat the Spaniard's engraved helmet. "I'm sorry I can't do as much for you sometime."

Lurching across the cabin floor, the girl picked up a Winchester .45-70 leaning against one of Kern's packs. She worked the lever to put a cartridge into the breech.

Then, feeling secure now that she was armed, the girl headed out into the blazing sunlight, her eyes focussed on the dizzy, bottomless chasm of Ruby Crater.

She saw no trace of the two outlaws. Perhaps at this moment they were busy exploring the tunnel of the Spanish gold diggings which her slain uncle had found after decades of search.

"I've got to get back to the canyon — to Jerry and Daddy."

Picking up the trail which the outlaws had made in bringing her and the load of supplies to the cabin, Arlina Colter headed across a sloping bench in which low-grade rubies twinkled in the lava formation underfoot.

She was working her way through the rocks and brush which cut off her view of Golden Poppy Canyon, when she heard a low mumble of voices ahead of her.

Clutching the rifle tightly, Arlina Colter wormed herself into a rocky fissure between two gigantic boulders and sank to her knees, scarce daring to breathe. If discovered she would defend her life to the last shell in her rifle, but thought of shooting it out with Russ Kern sickened the girl.

Footsteps on gravel and the low voices faded in the girl's ears, as the two men headed in the direction of the cabin. Arlina did not dare emerge from her hiding place, or she would have discovered that the passing men were not Kern and Rayborne, returning to the cabin, but the Masked Rider and Blue Hawk hunting for her!

Wriggling her way out through the other end of the fissure, Arlina Colter raced through the screening chaparral and saw the gulf of Golden Poppy Canyon looming ahead of her, beyond the jumping-off place of the cliff brink up which Kern had carried her.

"When they get back to the cabin and find me gone they'll rush out here. I've got to hurry — hurry —"

Descent of the cliff was impossible without the rope ladder, so the girl went to work with feverish haste, dragging the end of the ladder to the cliff's edge.

Feeding the wooden rungs over the edge of the canyon, the girl raced against time as she paid out the ladder into the depths below.

Finally, when the two ropes connected to the pine-tree anchors were stretched taut across the ground, Arlina knew the ladder had reached the bottom of the canyon. She thrust the Winchester through her belt and, gripping the sturdy rope, lowered herself over the edge.

She was in an agony of suspense for fear

Kern would show up at the cliff top, during every moment of her descent down the breath-taking hundred-and-twenty-foot ladder. A prayer of thanksgiving gusted from her lips as she finally found her bootsoles on solid earth.

Hurrying toward the picketed horses belonging to the outlaws, Arlina gasped in horror as she nearly collided with the mangled corpse of Bonanza Collins. She tore her eyes away from the grisly sight before she noted the shattered arrow which had caused the Whiskey Gulch storekeeper's death-plunge.

A moment later, she had unpicketed one of the horses and was astride, reining about for her flight. Arlina's brows arched in astonishment as she saw the Masked Rider's black stallion, Midnight, and Blue Hawk's leggy *grulla* grazing at the edge of the chaparral.

"That must mean that our two outlaw friends are somewhere in the canyon," she panted huskily, as she sent the horse galloping down the steeply sloped pit of the gorge. "They couldn't have climbed up into Ruby Crater, because the ladder wasn't there."

Fifteen minutes later, Arlina Colter galloped around a bend in Golden Poppy Canyon to find her path blocked by a large group of riders, who had gathered about an oblong of rocks by the trailside which appeared to be a grave.

For a moment the girl believed she had plunged headlong into a group of Kern's henchmen. Then she saw her fiancé, Jerry Markham, racing forward out of the group to meet her.

" 'Lina, darling!" choked the buckskin-clad rider, clasping the girl in his arms as she slid from horseback.

"We thought you were dead and buried — that grave there has your name on a slab of rock."

The other riders looked on curiously as Zeb Colter lumbered forward. The girl, tears of happiness streaming down her cheeks, turned from Jerry Markham's arms to her father's.

"My little girl," sobbed the old prospector. "We give up waitin' on El Diablo Peak and come huntin' you. This is the marshal of Whiskey Gulch an' his posse."

Clasped in her father's ecstatic embrace, the girl looked past Jerry Markham to where Red Royce was striding up, followed by several of his saddle-weary possemen.

"Our friends the Masked Rider and Blue Hawk are back up the canyon, dearest," Arlina said to Jerry Markham. "Oh, I have so much to tell you. I've seen Ruby Crater and —"

The girl broke off, as she saw Jerry Markham flush guiltily and glance over his shoulder at Red Royce. Turning, Arlina saw a grin spreading on the marshal's lips.

"So the Masked Rider and his Injun pard are further up this canyon, eh?" chuckled the lawman exultantly. "That's good news, seein' as how them owl-hooters had give us the slip. I reckon you'll get the reward on them huskies' scalps for tippin' off my posse where to find 'em, Miss Colter!"

Chapter XII
Kern's Ace in the Hole

The Masked Rider halted as he caught sight of a log shed shack at the base of a lava slope directly ahead. The trail of Russ Kern and his men led toward the structure, which was apparently a dug-out with log walls and a roof made of sod and small rocks on a pole-rafter support.

"We better take it easy, Hawk," muttered the outlaw, cocking his .45s. "Don't see no sign of life, but Kern may be inside of it. Especially if that's the shafthouse of the Ruby Crater gold diggin's."

Separating, so as not to form a compact target for ambush bullets out of the cabin, the two outlaws approached the lean-to built against the slope. No sound came from within, as they worked their way from rock to rock across the open ground.

Blue Hawk gained the blind end of the cabin first, and skulked forward to the doorway. A moment later, he turned to the

Masked Rider, who was approaching the cabin from the opposite end, and waved.

"The house is empty, Señor. Kern and his amigo are not here."

The black-clad mystery rider strode forward, eyes scanning the slope above the cabin, his nerves tingling with suspense as he realized that even now, Russ Kern might be notching his gunsights for the kill.

Entering the cabin the two outlaws surveyed the pile of supplies which Kern's men had lugged inside the cabin. A moment later, they were startled to discover the Spaniard's skeleton bent over the crude table in the middle of the room.

Approaching the armor-clad bones, the Masked Rider perceived a detail which had been overlooked by Arlina Colter a few minutes previously: The skeleton clutched a black-tarnished silver goblet in one bony hand. Stooping to inspect the cup, the outlaw saw greenish crystals of arsenic adhering to the inside. The Spaniard had committed suicide by drinking poison! And the explanation for the deed the Masked Rider discovered, a moment later, when he spotted a brittle parchment under the skeleton's other hand. On it had been written in Castillian script, which the Masked Rider translated with difficulty:

I, Sebastiano, am dying of thirst in this hellish place. Padre Junipero has gone to the mission at Sonoma for help, since our rope ladder was broken by the earthquake. My companions died in the mine when it collapsed, and I Sebastiano, am alone in this waterless crater. The good padre is a week over-due. . . .

"This is one of the Spaniards who worked the gold mine originally, I guess," mused the Masked Rider. "The priest never got back, for his bones were those found by Hardrock Colter. He must have broken a leg on his way for help."

Blue Hawk shrugged, and his words snapped the masked outlaw back to the present:

"The señorita Arlina is not imprisoned here, Senor. Where do we look now?"

The Masked Rider walked over to the door, passing a pile of rope lying on the earthen floor near the table. At the moment the rope did not convey any meaning to the outlaw, for he was busy studying the double row of footprints which led off to the right of the cabin, and down the slope toward the rim of Ruby Crater.

"Kern went off this direction, pard," announced the outlaw. "He must be hunting the gold mine. Or possibly he took Arlina down to the crater and threw her to her death. He'd be about the stripe to do such a thing."

Like hounds in quest of a beast of prey, the two men followed the tracks down to the crater's edge. Their flesh recoiled as they peered into the vast abyss.

Through the haze, a thousand feet below, they saw the green grass which covered the crater floor, and trees of great size which were dwarfed by distance to resemble seedlings. The overhang of the crater brink kept them from seeing whether Arlina Colter's mangled body lay below.

Kern's tracks followed the crater rim in a general easterly direction, where the steep slopes led down to a flat bench which rimmed the crater brink.

A hundred yards along the crater's edge, and out of sight of the Spanish cabin, the Masked Rider spotted the black maw of a tunnel which had been hewn out of the rock. Muck piles, hauled out by long-dead Spanish miners, littered the bench in front of the tunnel mouth, and were now overgrown with grass.

"The lost ghost mine, Señor!" whispered Blue Hawk. "That is where Señor Kern has gone. That is where he keeps the muchacha

— if she still lives."

Pulses racing, the two outlaws crept forward through the spiny cactus which grew up to the gold mine's mouth. Then both men froze, as their ears caught the sound of human voices issuing from the black throat of the mine.

"That cave-in back yonder shows why them early Spaniards quit workin' the mine, Tex," came the voice of Russ Kern, funneling out of the tunnel like a voice from a barrel, hollow and booming. "Behind that cave-in will be the main vein of ore. Just look at the yellow stuff flashin' in the tunnel walls here."

The Masked Rider grinned as he heard boots scraping on rubble, just inside the tunnel entrance. He and Blue Hawk drew back out of sight, the Indian ready with bow and arrow, the Masked Rider's .45s jutting from his sides.

"We're rich, boss!" came Tex Rayborne's triumphant chuckle. "There ain't been nothin' like this since the days o' '49."

An instant later, the two killers emerged into the open, Russ Kern carrying a smoking pine-knot torch which they had used in exploring the tunnel. Eyes blinking in the dazzling sunshine which flooded Ruby Crater, the two criminals were unaware of peril as they turned and headed back toward the cabin.

"Hoist 'em high buscaderos!"

The Masked Rider's voice came like a saw on oak-knots, to halt the startled owl-hooters in their tracks. Russ Kern started to reach for a belted Colt, then checked his draw as he heard the triple click of the black-clad outlaw's .45s coming to full cock. At the Masked Rider's elbow, the stolid-faced Yaqui had a steel-headed arrow aimed at Tex Rayborne's chest.

"How in ——" Kern's voice croaked off in a moan as the Indian glided forward and jerked his six-guns from holsters.

A moment later, Rayborne was similarly disarmed. Kern's henchman seemed incapable of speech, his eyes bulging in despair.

"Bonanza Collins sold us out!" rasped the Whiskey Gulch recorder, his face livid with rage. "That's how the Masked Rider and this blasted Injun got past our guard."

Rayborne nodded grimly.

"No other way up here, unless Collins dropped that rope ladder to 'em!" commented the outlaw, finding his voice at last. "Well, what do you buckos aim to do with us?"

The Masked Rider backed off a pace, scrutinizing his prisoners appraisingly.

"Where's Miss Colter?" he demanded sharply. "Is she back in the mine? Is she still alive?"

Kern's hooded orbs flashed malevolently.

"What's it worth to you to find out, Masked Rider?" he asked craftily. "If I tell yuh where the girl is, will you give me and Rayborne a chance to clear out of Ruby Crater? We'll stake our hides against the girl and the gold mine. Is that fair enough?"

But Kern's hopes died, as he heard the Masked Rider laugh harshly.

"We'll find the girl, wherever you've hidden her!" he clipped grimly. "Start marchin', you two. We'll take these sidewinders back to the cabin, Hawk, and rope 'em up. Then we'll make a systematic search for Arlina. If we don't find her, we'll chuck Kern and his amigo into the crater!"

Despair numbed the hearts of the two killers as they were herded back along the crater rim and up to the log cabin. There, ushered inside with the Masked Rider's guns at their backs. Kern and Rayborne made the dismaying discovery that Arlina Colter was gone, her rope bonds lying on the floor near the chair where she had been held prisoner.

The two crooks glanced at each other searchingly, unable to fathom the girl's escape. The Masked Rider had had nothing to do with it, judging from the fact that he and the Indian were still hunting for her.

The Yaqui picked up the maguay ropes which recently had held Arlina Colter, and made quick work of tying up the two owl-hooters, slashing the rope in two parts with his sheath knife.

"We'll head down to the mine and locate the girl, Hawk," the Masked Rider said, when the two outlaws were stretched flat on their backs on the cabin floor, securely bound. "It's ten to one we'll find her there. If we don't there's ways of making Kern talk, I reckon."

So saying, the masked outlaw and his Indian partner left the cabin and vanished on their way back to the ghost mine.

"The girl made a gitaway, Tex," spoke up Kern finally. "She must have sneaked up on Bonanza Collins and salivated him. Which would account for the rope ladder bein' down, and the Masked Rider and the Injun gettin' up."

A quarter hour elapsed, during which the two outlaws strained impotently at their bonds. But Blue Hawk had done a thorough job of tying his knots.

Approaching footsteps and a mumble of voices reached the ears of Kern and Rayborne shortly afterward, and they resigned themselves to their captors' return. But a moment later, a shadow fell through the cabin door, and Russ Kern peered up to see the red-bearded face of Red Royce, the Whiskey Gulch marshal, staring down at him.

"The Masked Rider's got here ahead of us, all right!" announced the lawman, turning back to where his possemen, with Arlina Colter and her father and fiancé, were crowding about the door for a glimpse of the trussed-up outlaws. "Well, Kern, it looks like you've played out your string. Zebediah Colter here has told me how it was *you* who dynamited that stagecoach and killed old Hardrock, to get this mine."

Russ Kern writhed frantically in his bonds.

"It's a lie, Red!" whined the trapped recorder. "The — the Masked Rider blew up that Wells-Fargo wagon."

A cold laugh came from behind Red Royce, and Kern's assaying assistant, Shane Pendle, appeared beside the marshal. Unseen by Red Royce, the leering assayer winked at Russ Kern.

"For ten years I been workin' for you, Russ!" snarled Shane Pendle. "But I never knowed you was a polecat. If you didn't blow up that stage, how come you and Tex

Rayborne are here at the Ruby Crater Mine, when you were supposed to be in Sacramento? Answer that one, you dirty rat!"

Russ Kern licked his parched lips frantically.

"It ain't us you want, Red!" gasped the recorder from Whiskey Gulch, eyeing the rock-faced marshal imploringly. "The Masked Rider and his Injun pard are down around the corner east of here, lookin' over that Spanish gold mine. Dab yore loop on them rannies, Red, and you'll collect a big bounty."

Red Royce strode into the cabin and knelt to examine the ropes which bound the two criminals from his home camp.

"I intend to arrest the Masked Rider, in spite of what Miss Colter and her father try to tell me about them being *bueno hombres*," Royce said grimly. "I recognize them as being enemies of society, and I intend to turn them over to a hangman eventually. But I think you are responsible for Hardrock's murder, Russ Kern. You can consider yourself under arrest."

The marshal headed back to the door, where Kern saw Shane Pendle and the other possemen staring into the cabin.

"Kern and Rayborne will stay tied," Royce announced. "Come on, amigos. We'll corral the Masked Rider and that Indian — and don't forget they're desperate criminals and will shoot to kill if they have to."

Kern heard Jerry Markham and Arlina Colter arguing desperately on the Masked Rider's behalf, as the marshal strode grimly down the slope toward the gold diggings, turning a deaf ear to their entreaties.

Five minutes later, running footsteps approached the cabin and the two heavily-bound outlaws looked up to see Shane Pendle ducking through the doorway, a hunting knife glinting in his fist.

"You fellers are lucky I happened to be in Royce's posse, or you'd stretch rope when Royce got you back to Whiskey Gulch," the assistant assayer panted, as he knelt down between Kern and Rayborne. "Roll over on your bellies, pardners, and I'll cut you loose."

Chapter XIII
Spanish Gold Mine

Beside the mouth of the ghost mine which Hardrock Colter had rediscovered after centuries, the Masked Rider picked up the smouldering pine-knot torch which Russ Kern had used ahead of them.

"There are no footprints of the señorita leading into the tunnel, Señor," pointed out Blue Hawk, pointing toward the tracks leading into and out of the mine tunnel. "I am afraid that Kern threw her into the crater."

The Masked Rider fanned the torch until it burst into flame once more.

"I don't see why Kern would take all the trouble to bring Arlina up here and then kill her," the masked outlaw contradicted. "She'll be back in this mine, Hawk, or I miss my guess. Kern carried her in, which accounts for her tracks being missing."

Holding the blazing pitch-knot overhead, the Masked Rider groped his way into the cavern, whose quartz walls showed the marks of pick-axes wielded by Spaniards of an earlier day, before blasting powder had come into general mining use.

With Blue Hawk padding on moccasined feet closely behind him, the Masked Rider pushed onward into the tunnel. Water dripped from the rocky ceiling, sizzling on the torch. The air was fusty, indicating that the mine had no other exit.

"Arlina!" shouted the Masked Rider, pausing as they came to a fork in the cavern.

The girl's name was flung back in taunting echoes from the two pitch-black tunnels dividing before them.

"She could be unconscious, or gagged," the Masked Rider commented, when the echoes of his shout died away without answer. "Kern's tracks go up both forks, where he explored the mine. But dead-end can't be far."

They chose the right-hand fork, following it to its end fifty yards beyond, where the gold-bearing vein had evidently struck a fault in the rock structure.

Free gold glittered like spatters of yellow paint on the rock walls, catching and refracting the guttering flare of the torch.

"With so much rich ore here, it means the vein itself must have been crawling with gold," commented the Masked Rider.

"Hardrock Colter wasn't exaggerating when he wrote his brother that this was a bonanza."

They retraced their steps to the fork and took the other tunnel. This was longer, and zigzagged for a hundred yards into the bedrock. Shoring timbers were unnecessary, due to the firmness of the rock structure.

Hope leaped in the Masked Rider's heart as he saw objects looming up on the cavern floor, just beyond the flickering glare of his pine torch. But they did not find the object of their hunt, Arlina Colter.

Instead, they discovered two oaken kegs labeled "Black Powder — Handle with Care," a case half filled with fresh dynamite sticks, and a smaller box containing percussion caps and a coil of fuse. There was also a modern single-jack drill.

"These explosives were brought in here by Hardrock Colter, Hawk," explained the Masked Rider. "I remember in his letter to Zebediah, he mentioned having done some blasting to get ore samples for assay purposes."

Fifty feet beyond Hardrock Colter's mining supplies, the two outlaws were dismayed to find that the old mine had caved in, blocking the tunnel with rock.

The cave-in had not been caused by

Colter's blasting a few weeks past, for the fallen rocks were festooned with spider webs and slick with moss, watered from roof seepage.

The guttering torch picked out a pair of skeleton legs protruding from the pile of fallen rock, and the Masked Rider drew grim conclusions.

"An earthquake must have toppled in this rock on top of the Spanish miners, Hawk," surmised the black-clad outlaw. "That's why the Ruby Crater Mine was not worked out to its finish. This is the cave-in Sebastiano mentioned in his suicide message."

Blue Hawk sighed heavily.

"Señorita Arlina is not in the gold mine," the Yaqui reminded the Masked Rider. "It means we will have to make Señor Kern talk, no? And that may mean that we will have to take the bad news back to her father and Señor Markham that the señorita is dead."

The pine-knot torch was nearing the end of its pitch supply, and the two outlaws picked their way back to the main shaft and scrambled on until they saw the semi-circle of daylight blazing at its mouth.

An uncanny sense of peril seized the Masked Rider as he dropped the exhausted torch in the rubble. Blue Hawk, walking shoulder to shoulder with his partner, caught the same feeling that all was not well, as they emerged into the open.

The Masked Rider was reaching for a holstered gun — for no reason that he could define, because he knew there was no possibility of their prisoners' having freed themselves from Blue Hawk's bonds — when a harsh order lashed out from the cactus clump at his left: "Raise your arms, pronto! We got the drop on you!"

Hand paralyzed on gun butt, the Masked Rider glanced about in time to see Marshal Red Royce emerge from the prickly pears. Half-hidden by the spiny cactus behind the marshal, he caught sight of the crouched figures of Royce's possemen, waiting with drawn guns.

Panic shot through the Masked Rider in that instant, as he tried to fathom by what miracle the Whiskey Gulch lawman and his entire posse had been able to scale the cliff at the blind end of Golden Poppy Canyon. But they were here, bringing showdown which promised to spell the end of the Masked Rider's career.

Knowing that to resist or to attempt ducking back into the mine would bring a point-blank blizzard of lead, Blue Hawk and his masked companion slowly raised their arms.

A low cry sounded behind the redheaded marshal, and the Masked Rider's jaw sagged in astonishment as he saw Arlina and Colter and Jerry Markham step out of the cactus.

"We — we tried to stop Mr. Royce, amigo," husked out Jerry Markham. "But he won't believe that you two risked your lives to bring Russ Kern to justice."

Red Royce stalked forward and lifted the Masked Rider's .45s from their holsters, jabbing them into the waistband of his Levi's. Turning to Blue Hawk, the lawman frisked the Yaqui for concealed guns, but found only the Indian's sheath knife. Blue Hawk had left his bow and quiver of arrows back at the cabin.

"Don't get me wrong, Markham," defended the marshal. "The Masked Rider is wanted for a lot o' crimes which his good work in Hardrock Colter's behalf ain't goin' to nullify in court. It's my duty to arrest the Masked Rider and hold him for the Nevada sheriff who chased these men into California. As for the Injun — he's the same walloper who let Wayne Morgan out o' jail. Whether Wayne Morgan blowed up that stagecoach or not, I won't rest content until I've captured that cowboy."

Posse members, among them Zeb Colter, crowded about the two prisoners as Marshal

133

Royce reached in a hip pocket for handcuffs to manacle his prisoners wrist to wrist.

Dangling the iron bracelets in one hand, Royce holstered his gun while his posse members ringed in the two outlaws with drawn weapons of all descriptions. In all his peril-packed career, the Masked Rider had never faced a doom as sure as this.

"No lawman has ever been able to see the face behind yore mask, busky," commented Red Royce. "I reckon I'll git that honor."

The Masked Rider stiffened as Royce lifted his hand, intending to jerk off the domino mask. When he did, Royce would know, for the first time, that the Masked Rider was Wayne Morgan, the cowboy he had chased out of Whiskey Gulch and pursued so relentlessly during the past week.

But Red Royce's fingers did not touch the Masked Rider's black domino.

In that hushed moment, a gunshot rang out over Ruby Crater and a gagged cry came from one of the posse riders on the outskirts of the crowd.

Shot between the shoulder blades, the Whiskey Gulch citizen pitched forward against his fellows.

Royce whirled about, the others following suit. Then the posse stiffened as one, as they caught sight of Russ Kern standing at the edge of Ruby Crater, levering a shell into the breech of his Winchester.

Standing behind the escaped outlaw was Shane Pendle, who had slipped unnoticed out of Royce's posse to release his boss. A rifle blazed in Pendle's hands, and a slug hammered into the compact group of lawmen assembled in front of the lost gold mine to drop a second victim in his tracks.

Chapter XIV
Dynamite Threat

Pendle and Kern then sent a fast-triggered salvo in their direction, dropping one more posse member before they could gain the safety of the cavern.

"That dirty rattlesnake of a Shane Pendle double-crossed us!" raged the marshal. "I might 'a' known Pendle was in cahoots with Kern. He sneaked back to the cabin and untied Kern and Rayborne."

The Masked Rider stepped forward from the group of men who were cowering back inside the mine, out of range of the outlaw's fire.

"Royce, I don't have to tell you that we're in a tight spot," rasped the outlaw. "This mine has no exit. We're trapped without food, and Kern will be able to starve us. The only way any of us can escape alive from Ruby Crater will be for Kern and his two pards to be killed or captured."

Royce ran a trembling hand through his

shock of red hair. Panic was in the lawman's eyes.

"I have nothing to lose by bucking those killers," the Masked Rider went on. "I realize that a hang rope awaits me and my Indian partner, once you turn us over to the Nevada sheriff as you plan. How about giving me back my guns and letting me try to drive Kern and his men away from the Crater?"

Royce hesitated, his eyes probing into the masked man's.

"I feel like a yellow dog, lettin' you do somethin' I ain't got the guts to order any of my men, or even myself, to do," Red Royce gruffed. "But if you're game to try to pull us out of this trap, Masked Rider —"

With the words, Royce lifted the Masked Rider's .45 Colts from his waistband and handed them to the black-clad outlaw, butts first.

"Don't Masked Rider!" gasped Arlina Colter, from inside the ranks of the men in the cave. "Kern will just kill you."

But the Masked Rider was gone, heading out along the tangle of prickly-pear cactus, guns palmed for showdown.

Crouched low, the Masked Rider saw Pendle and Kern walking along the crater rim, rifles held ready for a glimpse of their trapped foemen.

Kern vented an excited yell as he saw the black-cloaked outlaw come out into the open, fifty yards away. Shane Pendle's rifle came up spitting flame, and only the fact that the Masked Rider had anticipated the fire and had flung himself prone on the ledge saved him from death as a .30-30 slug tunneled the space where his body had been.

Sprawled flat, the Masked Rider squinted down his gunsights and squeezed trigger, as Shane Pendle levered a fresh shell into his Winchester. Gunsmoke founted from the bores of the outlaw's .45s, and when it cleared, the Masked Rider saw Russ Kern staring at the sprawled corpse of his assistant assayer. Blood was trickling from a pair of bullet holes punched through the middle of Pendle's forehead.

The death of his partner seemed to wipe out Kern's will to fight it out, despite the fact that his Winchester out-matched the Masked Rider's six-guns at that range. Spinning on his heels, Kern set off at top speed in the direction of Golden Poppy Canyon.

Bounding to his feet, the Masked Rider saw Tex Rayborne leave the rocks a short distance from the Spaniard's cabin, and sprint toward the chaparral where Kern was heading.

Both outlaws were now out of the Masked Rider's limited .45 range. Turning, the black-clad gunman shouted toward the gold mine entrance behind him:

"Come on, amigos! We've got a chance now to reach the cabin. We can't be trapped as easily there, and we can use Kern's grub supplies in case of a siege. Maybe after dark we can outwit 'em, at that."

Royce and his possemen trooped out of the mine, accompanied by Zebediah Colter and his daughter, with Jerry Markham racing in the forefront at the marshal's side.

Triggering his six-guns at the fleeing killers, the Masked Rider saw Kern and Rayborne vanish into the chaparral which cut off his view of Golden Poppy Canyon. But the Masked Rider had no hopes that the two gunhawks would escape down the rope ladder. There would be plenty of bloodshed before they managed to leave Ruby Crater, the Masked Rider was sure.

Strung out in a long line, the posse members raced past Shane Pendle's corpse and dived into the log-walled cabin. Rifles began hammering from the ambush of the chaparral, and bullets whining past his head drove the Masked Rider into the cabin along with the others.

"This is better than being trapped in the mine, but not much," the Masked Rider panted, as he stared about at the men who nearly filled the shack to capacity. "At least, we have food supplies, if no water to drink."

Blue Hawk, once more in possession of his bow and arrows, headed toward the doorway to scan the slope below. The Masked Rider reached out to grip the Yaqui's arm.

"Don't show yourself, Hawk," warned the black-clad outlaw. "Kern and his partner will undoubtedly cover the doorway with their .30-30s, and they could mow down every man who tried to make a break out of here. All we can do now is wait for nightfall. Then we'll see what we can do about smoking out those two buskies."

Night fell over Ruby Crater, filling the vast chasm with inky blackness. But a silver-dollar moon lifted above the Sierra Nevada crags to eastward before the sunset glow had spent itself, and the Masked Rider, taking charge of the bayed possemen inside the cabin, issued orders for everyone to keep inside.

Over in the chaparral near the rim overlooking Golden Poppy Canyon, Russ Kern and Tex Rayborne were holding a council of war. In spite of the unlucky turn of events which stemmed from Shane Pendle's death, the Whiskey Gulch recorder was optimistic.

"Forgettin' the gold mine for the time bein', we got to remember that our lives depend on keepin' Royce and the others inside that cabin," Kern said. "If one of 'em breaks out o' Ruby Crater, our fish is fried. We're only two against nearly twenty, Tex, but I think we can hold our own."

Tex Rayborne, squatting behind a moon-gilded boulder with his Winchester sights trained on the black door of the Spanish cabin across the clearing, shrugged.

"Don't forget they got our food supplies," he pointed out. "Susanville is the nearest place where we could get grub, and it'd take three days for one of us to make the round trip. We got to figger some way to lick them buskies before tomorrow, boss."

Kern rubbed his jaw reflectively. "I think I got a scheme that'll do it," he said thoughtfully. "Remember that blastin' powder and dynamite of Colter's over in the mine tunnel? We could blast the hull outfit out o' here with them explosives."

Rayborne grunted, squinting at the moon.

"How can we get over to the mine and get that dynamite?" he asked. "Don't forget the Masked Rider and the marshal are dead shots. They'd pick us off as we headed along the crater rim below the cabin."

The moon wheeled into a fleecy cloud-nest at that moment, and Russ Kern made up his mind.

"It'll be dark for a few minutes, till the moon sails out from behind them clouds," Kern said. "You keep guard on that cabin door, amigo. I'm goin' after that dynamite."

Disregarding Rayborne's protest, Russ Kern laid aside his rifle and burrowed his way out of the chaparral.

Stooped over, Kern raced out into the open, knowing that the reappearance of the moon would throw him into sharp relief, a sure target for the fire of the men trapped in the cabin.

But two minutes later Kern had reached the shelter of the gold mine, having crossed the open space below the cabin without having been seen.

Scratching a match, Kern fired a bundle of dry brush for a makeshift torch, and headed into the mine tunnel.

Soon he was standing before Hardrock Colter's cache of explosives.

By the light of the burning packet of brush, Kern worked with feverish haste. Lifting one of the oaken kegs of blasting powder, Kern broke open one end of the cask against a sharp rock, and dumped out the black contents.

Then he filled the empty keg with sticks of dynamite from the opened case nearby, stuffing the keg full. That done, Kern tucked the dynamite-laden keg under one elbow, picked up the smaller box containing a coil of fuse and percussion caps, and hurried back outdoors.

Moonlight streaming through a rift in the cloud bank gave Kern light enough to fit a detonation cap to the end of a strip of dynamite fuse, which he cut off short with his pocket knife. He thrust the capped fuse deep inside the sticks of dynamite in the keg, leaving only a few inches of the fuse projecting through the opened end of that keg.

That done, Russ Kern waited for the moon to plunge behind the clouds once more. When it did, almost total darkness obscured the landscape.

Kern had worked out the details of his murderous plan to wipe out their enemies inside the cabin, by the time he had reached the open ground once more. He was fully aware that a shaft of moonlight breaking through the clouds would expose him to the merciless fire of the bayed possemen, but he was gambling for high stakes: His life, against the riches of the Spanish ghost mine.

Reaching the base of the steep slope at the foot of which the Spanish miners had built their log-walled abode against a shallow dugout, Kern started climbing. By the time the moon came out again the recorder was out of sight of any sharpshooter peering through the cabin door. Kern was thankful that the cabin was not equipped with windows or loopholes of any kind.

Digging his boots into the rubble, Kern worked his way along the slope fifty yards above the cabin, until he was directly above the sod roof of the structure. Inside, he could hear voices as the trapped inmates discussed their predicament. The moonlight gave Tex Rayborne ample illumination to guard the cabin door against an attempted escape.

Seating himself on the steep slope, Russ Kern struck a match and ignited the end of the fuse. It started sputtering, throwing sparks like an ignited firecracker.

A harsh chuckle blew from Kern's lips as he placed the oaken keg on the ground in front of him, lining it up with the flat roof of the aged cabin below him.

Then he released the explosive-filled keg, saw it start rolling down the slope. There was a chance that the keg would explode from the impact of hitting the cabin roof, blowing the cabin and its inmates sky-high. If not, the keg would plunge through the flimsy, time-rotted roof and the short fuse would do the rest.

CHAPTER XV
RUBY CRATER SHOWDOWN

Voice low and steady the Masked Rider was addressing his trapped companions in preparation for showdown.

"Here's the set-up, amigos. Kern and Rayborne are ambushed between us and the getaway ladder leading into Golden Poppy Canyon. Their guns will cover this door. But if a few of us can get outside, we can scatter their fire enough to give us a chance to smoke them out. It goes without sayin' that they'll tally one or more of us, but it's the only way left."

The Masked Rider turned to Blue Hawk, who was squatting in the darkness near the table.

"I'll wait for the moon to go under a cloud, and then I'll duck through the door first," the outlaw said. "If I'm dropped by a lucky shot, you will make the break next, Blue Hawk. Next in line will be you, Royce, and then Jerry Markham. Don't try flooding out in a group, or those drygulchers couldn't help slaughtering —"

Crrrash! The Masked Rider's words were drowned in a roar of sound, as a heavy object smashed into the flimsy roof overhead.

There was a splintering sound as time-decayed pole rafters gave way under the weight, and then moonlight streamed into the cabin as a hurtling missile tore through a gaping hole in the roof and crashed against the table about which they were grouped.

The table legs smashed to pieces under the impact, and the mysterious object rolled to the earthen floor.

For a paralyzed instant, all eyes were upon the oaken keg which lay on the floor, spotlighted by the pencil of moonlight flooding through the broken roof. The air was swimming with dust and débris, and chunks of sod were tumbling down through the break in the rafters, onto the heads and shoulders of the astonished possemen.

It was the Masked Rider who came to his senses first, and recognized the meaning of the fizzling sparks which jetted from the opened end of the cask.

"Dynamite!" yelled the outlaw, as realization flooded through him. "That keg's loaded with explosive. Kern rolled that keg down the hill to wipe us out."

Pouncing like a cougar, the Masked Rider reached out to grab the sputtering end of the fuse. But he was a clock-tick too late, for the blazing core of the fuse burned its way out of reach of his fingers, sputtering on inside the closely packed sticks of dynamite.

Thoughts raced through the Masked Rider's brain in the stunned heartbeat of time which followed. He was faced with a suicidal decision, but he made it without an instant's delay.

There was no chance to extinguish the fuse. At any second, the detonating cap on the end of the fuse might be touched off, and the resultant blast would snuff out every human life in the cabin, if Russ Kern's murderous engine of death was not removed.

Scooping the heavy keg up in his arms, the Masked Rider turned and leaped for the door. He had a vague recollection of hearing Arlina Colter scream, and of Blue Hawk shouting at him in frantic farewell.

Less than five seconds had elapsed since the dynamite-laden keg tumbled through the flimsy roof into their midst, when the Masked Rider's pumping legs carried him over the threshold and out into the brilliant moonlight.

A gunshot roared from the chaparral where Tex Rayborne was ambushed, and a .30-30 bullet slammed into the door jamb an instant after the Masked Rider's rush carried him clear of the outlaw's previously lined-up angle of fire.

Hugging the keg of dynamite to his chest the black-masked outlaw sprinted down the gentle slope in front of the cabin, knowing that the dynamite must be well clear of the structure, if his sacrifice was to result in the saving of innocent lives.

Rayborne's .30-30 was roaring its song of death, and slugs kicked gravel about the Masked Rider's legs. If one of the streaking bullets struck the keg in his arms, there would not be enough left of the Masked Rider's body to pick up with a blotter.

Fifty feet beyond the cabin, the Masked Rider lowered the cask gently to the ground, the sizzling of the fuse registering plainly in his ears. Then he started the keg rolling toward the brink of Ruby Crater with a push of his boot.

From the slope above the cabin, Russ Kern had opened fire with his six-guns. The trembling people inside the cabin saw the Masked Rider fling himself to the ground

— and then the bounding keg exploded, as the short fuse reached the firing cap.

BRROOM! An ear-shattering roar accompanied the blinding yellow blast of flame as the terrific bomb cut loose its lethal detonation. Splintered remnants of the sturdy hardwood keg hurtled skyward.

The terrific concussion of the blast sent a wall of air tearing at the Masked Rider's prostrate body, rolling him a dozen yards as if he had been a fallen leaf. Smoke and dust mushroomed out along the ground, to hide him from the shocked eyes inside the cabin. Red Royce and his men were jolted to their knees, as the old shack rocked under the detonation.

Like a black-shrouded ghost, the Masked Rider got groggily to his feet, his ear-drums tortured by the roar of sound. His dropping to the ground an instant after releasing the deadly keg had saved his life, for the flying barrage of loose gravel bursting from the spot of the explosion would have peppered his body to hashmeat.

Stunned, his senses numbed, the Masked Rider lurched along the ground, dynamite smoke smiting his nostrils. His Colt .45s were in his hands, and he was heading toward the chaparral where Tex Rayborne was hidden, knowing that he would be an easy target for the outlaw's 30-30, the moment the sifting pall of dust had cleared away.

Invisible behind the smudge of drifting smoke, Russ Kern had left his vantage point on the slope above the cabin roof and was sprinting for the safety of the chaparral where Rayborne waited, his eyes probing through the settling débris to locate the door of the cabin.

A moment later the Masked Rider caught sight of the Whiskey Gulch recorder, legging through the roiling dust like a phantom.

A glad cry burst from the masked outlaw's lips, but his aching ear-drums did not register the sound. Clamping his jaw grimly he staggered off at an angle to cut off Kern's retreat.

The recorder sighted the Masked Rider an instant later and skidded to a halt, whirling about with six-guns blasting flame and smoke.

A slug raked the Masked Rider's forearm, and the stab of pain revived his befuddled senses. Dropping to one knee, the black-clad outlaw threw down his Peacemakers in chopping motions, letting gunhammers fall as the barrels came level.

A gagged cry came from Russ Kern, as

one of the Masked Rider's slugs blasted into his stomach and another shattered his left wrist, forcing him to drop one gun.

Sick with pain, Kern broke into a run. But smoke and the agony of his wounds had ruined the outlaw's sense of direction, for he was headed, not for Rayborne's hideout, but straight toward the yawning chasm of Ruby Crater.

The Masked Rider, running in dogged pursuit, held his fire as he saw Kern lurch to a halt on the brink of the volcanic abyss. Horror twisted Kern's face, as he turned about to face the showdown which the Masked Rider was forcing.

The recorder's right arm struggled up, fighting the dead weight of the six-gun in his hand. Then, before he could squeeze the trigger, life drained out of his legs, and he toppled slowly backward.

The Masked Rider came to a halt on the edge of the chasm, in time to see Russ Kern topple into empty space. He saw Kern's bullet-riddled form plummeting downward, a dwindling shadow in the moonlight-filled crater as he hurtled toward destruction fully a thousand feet below.

Tex Rayborne came scrambling out into the open then, his smoking Winchester lifted to blast at the Masked Rider at point-blank range. But even as the masked gunman lifted his .45s to meet the new threat swooping down upon him, he saw Rayborne's rush checked, saw a feather-tipped arrow strike and stay quivering in Rayborne's chest.

As Rayborne collapsed in death, the Masked Rider twisted his head to see his Yaqui Indian partner, Blue Hawk, gliding up through the smoke. Behind the Indian whose bow had dropped the last survivor of Kern's gang, the Masked Rider saw the figures of Zebediah Colter and Red Royce and the others, pouring out of the cabin.

A new dawn came to Ruby Crater, to find the tired posse from Whiskey Gulch busy consuming the tasty breakfast which Arlina Colter had prepared for them, out in the open, from the grub boxes which Russ Kern had brought into the wilderness.

Red Royce threaded his way through the men and halted in front of the Masked Rider, whose bullet-nicked arm had been bandaged by Arlina Colter.

"It goes without sayin', Masked Rider, that I'd turn in my badge sooner than I'd press charges agin' you," the Whiskey Gulch marshal said. "And that goes for all my men. Any owl-hooter who would do what you done — pick up a dynamite keg that

153

might blow you to atoms at any minute — just to save the lives of the John Laws who had arrested you — well, you just can't be the black-hearted killer you've been painted to be."

Blue Hawk grinned happily as he saw the Masked Rider shake hands with Red Royce.

"Everything turned out *bueno,*" the outlaw admitted. "Zeb Colter's got a gold mine here that's legally his, seein' that his brother Hardrock found it. And it looks as if Jerry Markham's goin' to be Zeb's son-in-law as soon as they can get to Susanville and roust up a sky pilot to tie the knot."

Laughter went through the crowd, as they looked at the prospector's daughter, locked in an embrace with the buckskin-clad express rider.

"I didn't come up here lookin' for the Masked Rider anyhow," Royce went on. "I was lookin' for Wayne Morgan, a cowboy. But just for my own curiosity — did you and Blue Hawk rescue Wayne Morgan from my jail down in Whiskey Gulch that night?"

The Masked Rider met the full impact of Royce's eyes and shook his head.

"I admit Blue Hawk helped Wayne Morgan escape," the Masked Rider said. Then he added, truthfully enough: "But as for me — I had nothing to do with getting Morgan out of your calaboose."

Soon after, the Masked Rider and Blue Hawk made their way to the rope ladder which gave access to Golden Poppy Canyon. The posse members and the trio from Hornitas lined up along the rimrock of Ruby Crater, as the two mystery riders climbed down the ladder and walked out to where their horses awaited their return.

"Come and see Jerry and me after we get settled down to housekeeping in Hornitas, won't you?" called down Arlina Colter, as she stood between her father and fiancé, watching the black-clad rider of the outlands mount Midnight.

The Masked Rider and his faithful Indian companion swung their horses about and headed down the canyon. A moment before they passed out of view, they reined their horses about and reared them dramatically in farewell, returning the waves of the group skylined against the sky on the rimrock above.

"We'll keep that date, sometime, Arlina!" called back the Masked Rider. "We'll be plumb curious to know how Zeb makes out workin' that Spanish gold mine — as well as hearin' whether Red Royce ever catches up with Wayne Morgan!"

So saying, the two outcasts headed down

the trail stirrup to stirrup, and were lost to view. It seemed difficult to believe that the two horsemen were wanted men, always on the dodge. This morning, with the golden sunlight streaming down on them, they seemed to be as free as eagles on the wing.

That was the way Arlina Colter and the men she loved would always remember them.

ABOUT THE AUTHOR

Walker A. Tompkins, known to fellow Western writers as "Two-Gun" because of the speed with which he wrote, was the creator of two series characters still fondly remembered, Tommy Rockford in Street and Smith's *Wild West Weekly* and the Paintin' Pistoleer in Dell Publishing's *Zane Grey's Western Magazine.* Tompkins was born in Prosser, Washington, and his memories of growing up in the Washington wheat country he later incorporated into one of his best novels, *West of Texas Law* (1948). He was living in Ocean Park, Washington in 1931 when he submitted his first story to *Wild West Weekly.* It was purchased and Tommy Rockford, first a railroad detective and later a captain with the Border Patrol, made his first appearance. Quite as popular was the series of White Wolf adventures he wrote for this magazine about Jim-Twin Allen under the house name **Hal Dunning.**

During the Second World War Tompkins served as a U.S. Army correspondent in Europe. Of all he wrote for the magazine market after leaving the service, his series about Justin O. Smith, the painter in the little town of Apache who is also handy with a six-gun, proved the most popular and the first twelve of these stories were collected in *The Paintin' Pistoleer* (1949). Tompkins's Golden Age began with *Flaming Canyon* (1948) and extended through such titles as *Manhunt West* (1949), *Border Ambush* (1951), *Prairie Marshal* (1952) and *Gold on the Hoof* (1953). His Western fiction is known for its intriguing plots, vivid settings, memorable characters, and engaging style. When, later in life, he turned to writing local history about Santa Barbara where he lived, he was honored by the California State Legislature for his contributions.

We hope you have enjoyed this Large Print book. Other Thorndike, Wheeler, Kennebec, and Chivers Press Large Print books are available at your library or directly from the publishers.

For information about current and upcoming titles, please call or write, without obligation, to:

Publisher
Thorndike Press
10 Water St., Suite 310
Waterville, ME 04901
Tel. (800) 223-1244

or visit our Web site at:

http://gale.cengage.com/thorndike

OR

Chivers Large Print
published by AudioGO Ltd
St James House, The Square
Lower Bristol Road
Bath BA2 3SB
England
Tel. +44(0) 800 136919
email: info@audiogo.co.uk
www.audiogo.co.uk

All our Large Print titles are designed for easy reading, and all our books are made to last.